THRALL

THRALL

Kimberly Todd Wade

HADLEY
RILLE
BOOKS

THRALL
Copyright © 2010 by Kimberly Todd Wade

ISBN-13 978-0-9827256-3-4

Published by
Hadley Rille Books
PO Box 25466
Overland Park, KS 66225
USA
www.hadleyrillebooks.com
contact@hadleyrillebooks.com
Attention: Eric T. Reynolds

Cover illustration copyright © 2010 by Gregg Cestaro

For Kent

PART ONE

THE LION'S TOOTH hung from a sinew around his neck. He pressed it to his chest so that he could feel his heart beat through its enamel. The lion's puffed exhalations caressed the interior of his skull. He tilted his chin above the tall grass, and his nostrils dilated. He tasted the faintly thrumming blood of his wounded prey. The breeze against his cheek was the faintest pink, and the entire group turned in its direction. They followed the humming pink scent, while their ears pricked to every rustling not made by their own feet. They made easy distinctions between the individual footfalls of each member of their party and thus knew who walked behind or to the side of whom without having to look.

A large black bird dove into the tall grass. The warm red of its descent streaked through the sky like an arrow shot straight to the site of the carcass. The hunters shrieked and ran, waving their arms and stamping their feet with jubilation.

The birds squawked and flapped, arching their bald necks, but quickly tottered off and gamboled into weary flight. The lead hunter grabbed hold of the exposed ribs of the once wild beast and shook, hooing loudly. He clutched at the tooth around his neck then fell to all fours, snapping and snarling. He scrabbled around his kill, his mouth slavering as those around him cheered. When he had settled back on his haunches, gleaming with satisfaction, they came forward, drawing sharpened stones from their leather sacks. They set about the carcass, scraping its tough remnants of flesh. They sucked and chewed and licked their fingers where they glistened with fat. They felt the vibrations of the others' knives working through the bones. Through the stones and bones they felt the heartbeats of their fellows. Each beat its distinctive color in concentric waves that mingled in the air over the carcass. They made the color of the tribe.

They walked with scrap-filled sacks, retracing their path through the grass bent back with color traces that signified where each had stepped. They recognized all their signs with assurance. As they moved, the world bent and broke over their bodies, sound and scent spinning webs of sensations like spider silk. Unlike their sleeping sight, experienced in fluid hues, their waking sight was awash with scents and sounds that added dashes of color to every corner of the visual landscape. Their senses wove together a net through which smells left visible trails so that animals were seen not only where they stood but where they had been, and sounds could be traced to their origins with eyes as well as ears.

The spring where they stopped to rest was surging toward its peak, filling a pool a man deep and several across. It was flanked on three sides by tall, rounded rocks. Sunning lizards scurried into cracks at their approach, leaving green trails to mark their passage. The men crouched at the spring edge and scooped refreshment to their mouths in cupped palms while blinking at their wavering reflections, watching their colors move out over the surface of the water. Slaked, their leader paused to see the lion's tooth swung forward beneath the first gray hairs on his chin. He touched his cheeks and moved his mouth in silent hoo, then lifted his eyes skyward, where the sun was settling down to twilight. He straightened. The others, who watched themselves sip without thirst, noticed his movement and let the water drip from their hands. They rose and began to follow in the direction of camp but looked briefly back at their fellow, who hadn't budged from his vision in the spring. They continued on their way, heads shaking off their confusion.

The camp was not far. One in front hooed, and they all listened as a chorus of hooing sounded ahead. They laughed amongst themselves and walked slow, although they would have loved to run into the eager caresses that awaited them. Let them come. Let them come, their leader motioned with his hand palm downward. They hooed nonchalantly and heard the padding of approaching footfalls beneath the resounding hoos. Their grinning tribemates came into view. The faces of the hunters were kissed and stroked as they were divested of their sacks. The women patted the hunters' bodies, cupped their genitals and looked down the path they had come. "Where's one more?" "One more?" they asked and looked worried, but the hunters laughed, "Alone by the spring."

"Ah, the son of one who is dead," said one of the women.

"The one who sounds like hoo," said another, and she uttered it with slight descending tones that graded from blue to purple to all their ears; they knew immediately of whom she spoke.

They grinned their agreement over his unfortunate strange character and proceeded toward their shelter.

11

One youngster, never a mother, broke from their file and walked along the spring rim, placing her feet in the larger prints of the hunters, her toes to their heels; she felt the soft mud of the shore squish the sides of her feet purple and warm. Her mouth filled with the flavor of the mineral rich clay as her eyes followed the colored stripes of scent to where Hoolow hunched over his reflection. She lowered herself by his side and leaned back on her hands, extending her legs toward the spring. Her feet paddled the water, her knees turned inward. The ripples coursed over his face, making it shimmer with color, hers and his mingled together. The girl stood as he pushed awkwardly to his feet and took her outstretched hand. Their pulses at first conflicted in their palms but came into tandem as they walked the path along the spring's open edge to where it turned off onto a low, steady rise. Red rocks rose around them as they circled to the left, where the camp was already in darkness, the people having chosen a natural shelter oriented to catch the first morning light.

The fire leaped beyond the lip of overhanging rock; its smoke spiraled a frothing column that merged with the sky out of their eyes' reach. The warm pleasant odor of the girl subsumed in the smell of the tribe that was like the clay dried and aerated to their nostrils as his feet plied the friable earth with shuffles. She let go of his hand and joined the women in humming as they folded ribbons of meat onto wooden stakes. He sat with the hunters lolling amongst the children, who, happy to have them at their level, fondled their faces and tweaked their twists of hair while inspecting their necks for brittle flakes of blood they might reconstitute with their tongues. The men tickled the children to make them laugh, and when the women tried to pass them laden stakes to hold over the fire, they refused, saying, "No, full," and patting their still hollow bellies.

"The animal was huge." The hunters' hands stretched to either side, fingers extended.

"The lion tore it to pieces with its claws." Growls to make the children squeal.

"The hunters feasted, and these scraps are all that are left."

A woman eyed the one closest to her and poked her thumb into his flat abdomen, "These ones," she grazed her finger over the lot of them, "must have stopped along the way home then," and all who heard burst with laughter. One hunter rolled onto his back with mirth, and a child promptly pounced on his belly, making him "oof" and fart simultaneously. Their laughter escalated to a fine and thrilling pitch that echoed through their three-walled chamber and projected over the plain. Hoolow felt himself convulse to their meter, but he was eyeing the pile of nuts cascading to the floor at the back of the shelter. His mouth watered at the thought of their rich mellow flavor. The others could not hear his stomach rumble above their din. To him it sounded a clear inner torment. It was easy for the others to refuse the offered meat. He was the only man of his age, a still growing man, who felt his hunger acutely. Although he had gorged the most at the corpse, he remained the thinnest. They could rub their bellies somewhat contentedly as they watched the women consume the scraps. They waited for their genitals to swell before choosing the consorts they attempted to lead away from the fire to a privacy thwarted by a passel of following children.

The two women who had sucklers stared into the mesmerizing flames. One began to "ooo" softly to the flashing rhythm. She rocked, front to back, the naked little one tucked to her belly. The others responded to her vocalization. They leaned toward the fire, attempting to join their vision with hers. They watched the flames throw off sparks that

13

danced trails colored by the mother's tones. They joined in the singing, matching her pitch and flow. The ones behind bushes hurried back with the children following at a safe distance, and all settled around the fire. They sang in lilting vowels that soared and fell by internally guided degrees. Hoolow sang as he watched the tracers of color crisscross above the flames until he was distracted by thoughts of the girl, who sat close to her mother and younger sister. He looked to her, her face shiny and flecked with colors that swirled about her half-closed lids. He thought of himself then, remembering the clumsy way he had risen from the side of the spring to take her hand. She had stood gracefully, coated in skin with the shade and sheen of a doe's. Her wide-set eyes were likewise limpid and black. He lost all sight of the dancing colors as he summoned his own slight image to stand next to the muscular forms of the other men. If only, he thought, the women would throw some of the nuts on the fire, and he reveled in the imagined smell of their roasting. He could hear them crack in the hungry silence. His imaginary hand reached to snatch one from the embers, to peel its crackled skin and expose the pale flesh as good as meat, when it dawned on him that all was not as quiet as his thought's projection. In fact there was a sound, the sound of a single blue voice singing—and it was his! He looked at the faces all watching him. They'd been drawn into this intense observation by his incomprehensible failure to sing in tune and his continuation of the loathsome atonality after they had fallen off in wonderment. When he stopped, his face stricken with humiliation, they laughed and slapped their thighs at this most appropriate response. He could always be counted on for unintended comedic effects, and it was with the utmost affection that some tried to imitate his off-key notes, but they couldn't keep from falling into harmony with one another and were soon entranced, while Hoolow focused hard at blending his voice with theirs. Although he had laughed with them, he'd felt a bitter hurt, a lingering sting that threatened to draw his attention away again. Eventually their song petered as sleepers dropped off. The first ones crept deeper into the shelter to claim the hip-cradling depressions carved into the hard-packed floor. The lingerers settled by the fire. Hoolow made sure not to be the last singing, although he only pretended to sleep sitting up next to the fire. Really he watched the girl scoot to her mother's curved back, her little sister already curled against the maternal belly.

The people awoke at the first light that streamed into their natural shelter, adumbrating the dusty bodies that had been clumped together in slumber. Women picked the specks from their eyes and set about inspecting the skins of their children in the fresh light. Hoolow was awakened by sounds of muttered protest rather than by the light, which failed to penetrate his fitful sleep. He sat up, immediately annoyed that the women dallied in getting the nuts to the fire. He tried to hide his hard-on while rising despite no one paying him the slightest attention, being all consumed by their own ritual scratchings and twistings to relieve the tension of sleep. He trailed away from the shelter in the opposite direction from which he had come from the spring, and finding a shrub of ample size, stooped to claw out a hole in which to defecate. He squatted, and as the smooth solid turds slid from his rectum, he admired the pinkening sky. A good mood rose with the steam. Refreshed, he hurried back to the smell of roasting nuts, eager to reserve his portion.

Their fingers skinned the nuts, and while they chomped the mealy flesh, pausing to nibble herbs between mouthfuls, one of the young hunters stood to tell his dream. He held his shoulders back with impressive symmetry; his toes pointed to the simmering fire. The aura of a woman's scent intensified his hypnotic power. "There is a bull, a big young animal. Its fur lies all in one direction over its body so sun gleams off of it." His hand slid horizontally through the air, delineating the contours of the beast's back. "It grazes through the tall grass, inattentive because it knows none dare attack it. Its horns are long and sharp, angled for defense." The young hunter raised his arms bent at the elbow and leaned over at the waist so that his torso became the powerful neck of the bull. He worked his mouth over the invisible grass and shook his head to tear it free from the earth. "As it crops unaware, it steps too near a snake. The snake rears and strikes above the hard part of the foot." He kicked back his right foot and shook it. His audience watched the rippling body of the snake arc through the air. "The bull runs. It is strong." The young hunter stomped around the firepit, emphasizing the bull's power, its speed harder to demonstrate within the confines of the shelter. "But the wound festers." The young hunter raised his right foot and held it against his left calf. His face showed his brave pain. "Dogs smell the pus from miles away." He dropped his horns and brought his hands to the sides of his head with thumbs folded into palms. He rotated his new ears, capturing sounds from all directions. He raised his long snout to sniff the air. "The dogs click jaws and follow the scent through the grass. The bull is there. The dogs circle." The dream teller whirled between acting the part of the bull and an entire pack of dogs. "A young dog leaps and bites. Then all the dogs attack." It was no longer necessary to mimic the animals' shapes as his tribemates were engaged in envisioning the scene. "The bull can't run on its wounded foot. Now dogs are hanging on every part of it. It can't run. It must fall." He lost himself in the struggle and roiled across the floor of the shelter, beating off dogs while at the same time using their jaws to attack. "The dogs tear meat from its bones." He sat up blinking, triumphant.

As the people watched, the starch dissolving in their mouths assumed the flavor of blood, but to the tongue of the gray-bearded hunter the rich metallic taste was backed with sour. He surveyed the other hunters transfixed by the dream teller, their ears already growing long and pointed, their skins mottling. He was the last dog in the pack, and he felt a quiver shoot through his speckled flanks. The flashing sharp hooves of the bull dashed around him as he hung tenaciously to its withers. When its front knees buckled and its head slumped to earth, its back legs would still be thrashing. The graybeard could not change his position, but he would have his own story to tell when the hunt was over, one that could only raise his esteem with the tribe. He rose to his feet in well-practiced ignorance of the pain that pounded from hip to ankle. He cupped his hand to his ear, saying, "The stones are calling."

The other hunters tilted their heads in concentration. "Yes," they nodded one by one. The women eyed them suspiciously.

The men gathered their spear shafts, while the women pretended to laze about, combing their fingers through each other's hair. They would wait until the men were out of sight before donning the slings that served as hampers for the vegetables they collected. Their work would be done before the men reached the quarry.

The sun hung at its zenith, and the men periodically spoke to each other, "The stones are calling loudly today."

"Yes, loudly."

There was always agreement, except from Hoolow, who heard nothing and thus stayed quiet. He envisioned the level of nutmeat in his stomach dwindling as it trickled down into his intestines. His stomach would be empty by the time they reached the quarry, as their ritual path circumnavigated their goal, enticing the stones' voices to cry out louder and louder for the hunters. Hoolow had given up trying to hear, although he sometimes tilted his head in imitation of the others. They appeared to be fooled.

An outcrop of boulders rested on the plain, their gray shoulders humped heavenward. The hunters approached, and following the graybeard's lead, laid their hands against the boulders' weathered skin. The great stones sent subtle vibrations through the men's palms, but they didn't speak in words. The graybeard intoned, "These are only the sisters of the ones who are calling. The sisters cannot give permission."

The hunters moved off, and Hoolow watched them trail ahead as he stood with his hand against the giant rock. By hard concentration he could just make out the vibration coming through the stone, but was it any different from the vibration he felt from the earth, that which travelled up through his feet? His inability to distinguish between the two troubled him, but he hurried on to catch up with the other hunters.

They passed by a shelf of rock with an opening like their shelter, but there was no wall to be seen at the back; this one extended on into blackness. The graybeard turned to Hoolow and repeated in ritual fashion, "Never go into the black cave. Animals without bodies live there. They will try to steal a body."

The other hunters looked fearfully at the cave opening as they were meant to do. Hoolow copied their expression, but it did not penetrate him with the concomitant emotion as it did the others. Moments later they were back on their round to the quarry, and the voices of the stones made them forget their fear, but Hoolow was fixated on the bodiless animals. What would an animal without a body look like? How would it feel to have such a creature inside his body? Would he control it or it him?

18

The grandmother rock stood alone and leaning, her giant bulk suspended over the plain at an impossible angle and without the benefit of a stick. The graybeard stood in front of her and raised his headless spear. The others stood at a respectful distance as he spoke, "The sons and daughters are calling, can the people go to them?" In unison the men stepped forward and laid a hand to the rockface. They nodded their heads. The vibration Hoolow felt was no different from that of the sisters. He followed the others on their final leg to the quarry.

The quarry was once a vast smooth extrusion from the earth. It had cooled by gentle uncracking degrees, producing a slippery rock that broke with sharp edges, only shattering over a vein that had once been molten froth. Chunks from the brown band in the lighter colored rockface crumbled to the ground over millennia and called to the hunters, who stepped reverently over the layers of chips that represented the debris of thousands of spearpoints chiseled by generations like themselves. Only Hoolow was mysteriously different in his inability to learn the craft.

For a brief period in early childhood he'd seen as the others saw, heard what they heard, but then the visions, compressed by the heat of individual thoughts, seemed to melt out of his awareness. The visions became spare fragments encountered in unsuspecting moments. If he was relaxed, as just before sleep or when his senses were numbed by a repetitive activity he was not bored by, then the visions and voices fell upon him and were of no use as they would be for knapping flint, when he concentrated on calling them forth. As an older child he'd imitated; his desire for the voices fooled him into believing he heard them speak—"Not this one," "This one"—as he was told they spoke. His mistakes made him realize his error.

He picked up a rock and split it as he'd been taught, but without listening. The rock had a fault that caused it to shatter into random pieces, none suitable to any purpose.

The graybeard admonished, "Listen, the rock will tell of its flaw."

Hoolow resigned himself to the fact that he was not a good flintknapper. He hadn't the innate skill required. He was left alone with his fumblings, while the others became absorbed in their tasks, listening intently to the instructions the stones whispered through their hands as they were turned. They made their strikes with hammerstones, detaching the pocked cortex to reveal immaculate interiors. The voices became more specific, the flakes asking for removal smaller, saying, "Here," their shapes highlighted in white against the caramel color of the chert. Spearheads began to emerge.

The girl walked unhurriedly through the blurred sounds of calling plants—"Eat," "Don't eat." She made her way to the quarry by a different route, a woman's route unknown to the men, just as their route with its boggling convolutions was unknown to the women. Her blood pulsed a blue high note, then whooshed low. She cocked her ear to the voices of the stones; their words, faint and cracking, grew louder at her approach, but no clearer of meaning. The mystery didn't trouble her.

Amongst the looming rocks she saw the backs of the men bent to their work, the stones barking commands. There was one who fumbled with the stone in his hands. It refused to speak no matter how he cajoled, and the girl could sense his frustration from where she crouched behind a bush. She chose her moment to stand, waiting for his squeezed shut eyes to flicker open in her direction. Her calculation was correct, and her gesture caught his attention. The stone tumbled from his grip, and he moved to her like a somnambulist. Behind the bush she lay reaching up to him with all four limbs, and he allowed himself to crumple into her grasp. Her body moved like a wave beneath him, drawing him in, as her teeth gently latched to his shoulder, transmitting rhythmic grunts down his spine to mingle with the moist electricity of her groin joined with his. Flashes of colors succeeded one another too fast for comprehension until he opened his eyes to the calming blue of sky. The girl propped herself on an elbow and leaned over him to draw her hand across his cheek. They shared smiles, and he felt himself fall into the serene blackness of her eyes, sensing a depth he could tumble through without ever reaching bottom. She blinked, when he touched her cheek. She got to her feet, and the dust from her body fell into his eyes. He rubbed against the sting. When he could open them again, she was already turned from him and taking her first step away. He groped for her heel as it was lifted by the felicific arch of her foot. It slipped from his fingers, and the girl looked down on him from over the shiny slope of her shoulder. Still smiling, she went on her way. Hoolow was too overcome by the loss to call out, but the distress throbbed away, leaving in its wake a shadow of the serenity that had enveloped him as he gazed into her eyes. He sat on his heels, looking in the direction she had gone.

The other men had finished their conversations with the stones and were dilatorily assembling the makings of a fire. When Hoolow emerged from behind the bush, they smirked and grinned, and Hoolow felt angry at them without understanding why. He returned their smiles and settled with them by the fire, where they twisted tough fibers of grass into the twine they would use for attaching their fresh spearheads to their shafts. They hummed as they wound the fibers between forefinger and thumb, sinking into droolingly meditative stares while Hoolow was distracted by the

21

convulsive grumble of his belly. They had collected no food, although within sight of the quarry were many edible species. He would like to pick and eat them, but it was forbidden for men to do so. He'd picked and eaten them as a boy, and the memory of the succulent green shoots fresh from the earth to his mouth made him salivate. But they must be hungry for the hunt. The hunger will make them better hunters. He resented the hunger that he could satisfy with a handful from the earth, nonsensically forbidden to him. Why, since the women picked with their hands, which were the same as a man's, and not their vaginas? He felt angry again, but soothed himself with an image of the girl's fine hands. They were not like a man's. And it had been a long time since he'd picked with the women. What if they did use their vaginas? He pictured them squatting over plants and laughed.

Shocked out of vacuity, the others turned to him. "What vision?" asked the graybeard.

Hoolow shook his head and walked from the fire as if he needed to urinate, which he did, looking up at the stars. He felt soothed when the stars started to swirl above him. Faint traces of color in their spinning seemed to confirm that his vision was like the others. In his relaxation, the stars' distant chimes caressed his ears, and he hurried back, eager to elaborate on the song for his fellows.

But upon his return to the fire, he could see that they were already engrossed by the shadows projected on the walls of the quarry. His momentary sense of fellowship fleeted away to the sounds of their exclamations at the images they saw.

"There!"

"Look there!"

"Ah!"

They roared and snarled as Hoolow threw himself down by the fire and sulked for his own benefit, but he couldn't keep the others' words from reaching him. He tried not to pay attention but could not keep his eyes from squinting at the shadows.

Black shapes took on the forms of their descriptions. They grew the appropriate appendages: legs and snouts and bristles. They stepped away from the wall in color, full of vigor. They stomped and rooted in the quarry dust, while the hunters hooed their delight. A different teller pointed to the rabbit that flashed out of a crack as flame flickered over it. Everyone turned to it at once, even Hoolow, although he didn't startle at its sudden bounding. The others laughed in surprise. Hoolow fell in with them; it felt good to share their mirth. As the next teller lifted his hand to sculpt a new beast out of the shadows, Hoolow paid close attention. The rest flinched away from the roaring cat. Hoolow watched the shadows shift in a wave of licks. It resembled the long fur of a lion in mid-run. He could imagine the rest, but by the time the full vision prowled through his head, another teller was spouting a new description to which the others reacted instantly. He fell behind until he gave up trying, but amidst all the laughter it didn't seem so important. The graybeard leaned forward, his face almost touching the ground, and he grabbed onto Hoolow's thigh for support. The warm pressure of his hand linked Hoolow to the rest. The reverberation of the graybeard's laugher shot through their connection, and Hoolow felt the combined tremble. The sense of union lingered after the disengagement, when the graybeard conjured a new pig from the wall. This one chased the young hunter around the fire until he dropped into submission and mimed being devoured alive by the swine's blunt teeth. By the time the others recovered from the hilarity of this scene, the fire had died down to a line of grasshoppers. All were too tired to build it up to something more aggressive. The others noticed the graybeard's eyelids at half-mast, and their own lids slipped to the same level. In another instant they fell into simultaneous slumber. Hoolow, feeling himself in the embrace of his comrades' shared consciousness, slept, too.

In the morning the young hunter announced, "The bull has slept under a tree."

The other hunters arose eagerly, but Hoolow's stomach pained him to distraction. He picked up his spear shaft, to which the graybeard had attached a point of his own making, and desultorily followed the others. At first he nursed his discomfort by noting every edible plant in their path, but as the heat intensified, he allowed himself to fall in step with the others. They moved as a single unit, rendering his independent thoughts superfluous. He let them melt away. His senses receded to the narrow focus of placing his feet in the prints of the ones in front of him, only touching the grass they'd already touched as he brought up the rear. When the front stopped abruptly, he plowed on, causing a ripple of bumping that nearly knocked their leader, the young hunter, off his feet, disrupting the dignity of his straight posture with long arm extended. The young hunter regained his balance and looked to Hoolow, but seeing his mortification, only emitted a yelp of laughter before training his eyes back to the tree. He traced over its lopsided canopy, comparing it with the one in his dream. He was not convinced it was the same, but it was similar and appropriate for further investigation. He motioned to the others over his shoulder, and they proceeded.

The tree stood at the top of a gentle incline they felt in their thighs as they forged ahead, the grass thinning in their path. The young hunter knelt to examine a track; detecting no difference in the color of the soil within and without its sphere, he moved his hand over it, feeling the consistent texture of the dirt—an old track. He stood and squinted again toward the tree, now closer and viewed from a different angle. Convinced it was the one, he moved faster in its direction.

By the time they reached it, its shade puddled beneath the branches. Tracks crisscrossed around its base, and the hunters spread out to determine which were the most recent. Hoolow pretended to look like the others, but he did not understand their methods. To him, the trunk was rubbed smooth all the way around, but the graybeard ran his hands over the bark and plucked from it a tuft of fur. Bringing it to his nostrils, he sniffed and nodded. The scent of the animal was bright red, fresh. Meanwhile the young hunter paced off a large depression in the grass, well to the west of the current shade. The animal had rested in the long shadow of morning. On his hands and knees, the young hunter circled and sniffed, but the traces were an impossibly overlapping welter. Where the shorter grass gave way to the longer, he examined the breaks halfway up the blades. He snapped a blade between forefinger and thumb and compared the new break to the others. His impressions were vague. It was creeping passed midday, and the bull had left the scene early in the morning, allowing ample time for the grass breaks to dry evenly in the sun.

The graybeard watched the young hunter make his determinations. He had his own sense of which direction the animal had taken, but he stayed quiet and eased his back against the tree. The others soon joined him, crowding into the shade, each facing out in another direction. They sat for some time, none speaking, until the young hunter rose, picked up his spear and walked straight. The others scrambled to follow, the graybeard smiling and Hoolow confused and hungry.

His mouth, too, was dry. When he thought about it, his feet hurt, and the sun beat his shoulders. On another day they may have sat beneath the tree all afternoon. They may have slept there through the night. Hoolow followed the other's designs, whether they were the graybeard's or the young hunter's meant nothing to him. They both seemed moved by the same force, one unhampered, possibly enhanced, by hunger.

Sunlight was moving horizontally across the plain when the young hunter unshouldered his spear. "There is far to go tomorrow," he said.

They would make camp in the open. The others relaxed, put down their spears and empty sacks and began preparations for a fire. It was soon assembled, and there was nothing else to do with the remaining hour of twilight. Hoolow kicked the dirt around the perimeter of their camp. He forced his thoughts away from his hunger, and they fell to the girl. Warm feeling flooded him, but it was tempered by anxiety. She had left so soon after their encounter—had her satisfaction been incomplete? He reconstructed the image of her last look, down and over her shoulder. No, it had been a look of perfect happiness. He smiled to himself.

The graybeard noticed the change in Hoolow's expression and dug an elbow into the ribs of the young hunter sitting next to him. When he responded with a questioning look, the graybeard inclined his head toward Hoolow, whose face contorted to a series of unprovoked emotions. His observers clamped their hands over their mouths and gestured to the others until all watched Hoolow contemplate further interactions with the girl—making her laugh, making her squeal with delight over the choicest piece of meat, comforting her after watching her rise naked from the spring and cut her neat little foot on a sharp rock—but every constructed vision was somehow unsatisfying, not expressive enough of the depth of his feeling. Of their mutual feeling. He paused his pacing next to a shrub from which he snapped a branch. He twisted it with the undefined intention of making something of it, something he could give to the girl that would be of his own hand and therefore the only manner of thing with which he could hope to express himself. He struggled to see some kind of shape in it, he knew not what, but the others always talked of things they could see, when he could only see rocks and trees and sky, except when out of sheer concentration, he imagined that he saw as they did, but how could he be sure that his vision was the same?

The others dropped their hands, fascinated by the sight of him peeling the bark from a useless stick. Should they tell him it was not the right kind?

Hoolow looked at them and saw that he was being watched, but he did not desist from his activity, for if he gave up on the stick he would have no other recourse but to go and sit with them. The rest are sure of each other, he thought, turning his head back to his hands. He needed to be sure of himself. He bent the stick into a series of angles that looked like nothing. His manipulations grew more aggressive until the stick broke in two, the smaller half falling at his feet. He growled and kicked it, and lifting the other piece above his shoulder, threw it with all his might, not waiting to see it land before turning toward the fire. It was near dark and not difficult to avoid making eye contact.

The others were curious of Hoolow, but the graybeard asked the young hunter to repeat his dream of the hunt, which he obliged with alacrity, captivating the others, who looked for new clues in his retelling. Finding none, they looked to the stars, whose glittering tinkled through the sky like the clinking of crystals. They turned their ears to the sound and questioned each other as to what the stars meant to convey, but this night their portents for the hunt were murky, too distant to make out, although they took turns walking a short distance from the popping fire to better distinguish the tones.

At dawn they woke Hoolow from a deep sleep so that he was still disoriented as they made their way to a nearby spring. The cool air revived him as he knelt with the others, skimming the surface of the muddy water with their cupped hands. He couldn't help but imagine the wide clear water of the spring near their shelter. The water here was not even enough for a good splash, and its thickness insulted his thirst. The graybeard, first slaked, scoured the soft mud around the spring for tracks. He straddled his discovery and hooed. He waited for the young hunter to gain his side before the two of them knelt to examine it, the others leaning over their shoulders. It had been made the day before and had solidified to a perfect, undisturbed casting, a good omen for their success. The sharp print delineated the right back hoof of a large bull, its tip sunk deep with little pressure placed on the hock, sure sign of an animal in pain and limping, just as in the young hunter's dream. They moved together in the direction the hoof pointed and had not gone far before spotting dust rising on the horizon, indicative of a herd of cows, but they were looking for a solitary male.

The graybeard suggested, "An injured animal wants to be near others of its kind."

They moved toward the herd. As the sun grew higher, Hoolow grew weary and distracted by his hunger until the animal they sought was pointed out to him. His senses trained with the others. They communicated by sidelong glances as they watched the bull crop grass, standing still with its back right hoof resting against the ground on its tip. The flesh shimmied over its flank as it flicked its tail at the flies. The hunters moved around to its other side, knowing it would have a harder time bolting from the right. The bull threw its head in their direction as they circled behind its rump. Each hunter froze in place, but the animal was only trying to dislodge the flies from its ears, which twitched manically for a moment before its head dropped back to cropping. The hunters crouched, prepared to strike, but just as the young hunter rose to make the first thrust, the bull took a step and stretched its neck for a new clump of grass. Rather than plunging to the top of the spine, the spear lodged in the shoulder. The bull bolted, demonstrating more power in the injured back leg than the hunters had thought possible. The young hunter's spear sheared against the bull's shoulder blade, ground by the massive muscle that had stood it upright upon impact. The others rushed out with spears ready to jab, but the animal moved so swiftly they were forced to reverse their grips for throwing. The graybeard, with his experienced reflex, was the only one whose spear made contact, but it didn't stick. It glanced off the rump, tearing loose a flap of hide that was pink on the inside. The dogs pursued at a gallop, barking and snapping. They were soon outdistanced. The hunters returned to the scene of attack and picked up their spears. They reenacted the scene in high theatrical style, each narrating simultaneously, adding barks and additional spear thrusts, each making numerous contacts with the beast. It in no way resembled the silent meditation of the actual strike, and Hoolow didn't understand it, but he participated, for a moment sharing in the exhilaration, the boredom of tracking relieved.

Allowing the animal to tire, they made camp on the spot and continued their celebration into the night. No sooner had stars appeared than great rain clouds gathered over them and poured down a hard flurry of invisible stinging pellets that sent up dry puffs of dust until the ground was saturated and streaming. They piled wood on the fire, trying to satiate its hiss, and pushed the brush they'd collected for reserve closer so that it might remain dry on at least one side. Into their general misery bolted an explosion of light; it rent the distant sky as if the sun were trying to tear through the skin of night. The darkness resisted by stamping the earth, and its rumbling footfalls echoed around them. They screeched in response and waved sticks, threatening the sun back into its slumber. Another crack and tear in the sky illuminated all the colors that were unnatural to night, and the hunters joined the darkness in stamping its resistance. They howled to the weakened sliver of moon obscured by its thick blanket of cloud, all except Hoolow, who huddled unnoticed beneath a briar. His fear shivers fed off the electric charges, and he struggled to hold himself still against the pricking thorns, only crawling out when the rain had subsided to a drizzle and lightning a far off crackle. The others idled next to their sizzling fire, hooing and huffing, unable to settle; they stood only to drop back to their haunches after a few paces. None paid any attention to Hoolow, who selected a prime spot next to the flames and reposed, turning over by degrees both drying his skin and coating it with fine dust in the same action.

In the morning the others blinked awake and were surprised to see innocuous white clouds scattered about the sky. They watched them drift to ever further corners and stood up, stretching and flexing. They looked at Hoolow still sleeping by the fire. They prodded him awake with their feet but did not bother to question him as to what dreams so beguiled that the light couldn't penetrate. While he was still rising, they shouldered their spears and headed in the direction of their prey. Hoolow cut short his stretching to catch up.

Humidity clung to the grass, and Hoolow felt the dust with which he'd unconsciously coated himself begin to slide across his skin, caking into the creases of his elbows and the backs of his knees. It was most bothersome where it rimed his neck and made him long to break from the pack to find a place to bathe. He resolved that should they pass by a lake he would douse himself, but when the unbelievable mirage appeared before them, he found himself unable to disengage from the other hunters. Their intensity bound them together like sap as they bent over the most recent spoor that was streaked with blood, its edges distinct and true, undiluted by the rain. It could not be very old. They moved together at a quicker pace, their excitement unvoiced but evident in the brilliant violet haze that enveloped them.

The beast lay under the scant shade of a listing tree. The sun beat over its heaving sides in patches. The hunters approached stealthily, but the animal's senses were heightened by pain, and it reared its head in their direction. The hunters fanned to either side, and the animal's eyes lost their focus in trying to track their disparate movements. They drew closer, spears lifting. The animal lunged, first to one side, then the other. It tried to orient its broad, sharp horns for attack, but the effort did no more than bare its neck, pulsating with panic. The graybeard plunged his spear to the lung, releasing a spew of bloody foam through the bull's nostrils. The young hunter stood behind the graybeard and aped his movement with his own splintered shaft. He was the real killer, and it was to him that the bull spoke, "Life is given." All but Hoolow heard the words that ameliorated any guilt they might have felt for the killing. While they listened, Hoolow watched the bright eyes of the bull dim. Its powerful body jerked and trembled against the release of its life, affording Hoolow a moment to contemplate its necessity before he joined the others in butchering.

When the graybeard pulled out his point, the young hunter rushed forward and knelt to press his mouth to the gushing slit, the tip of the bull's horn crooked inches from his cheek. He sat back when the blood had gone to a trickle and joined the others in bracing against the bull's side. When its belly was exposed, they worked it open with their sharpened stones and dug in their hands to pull free great coils of guts. While the graybeard reached deep to release the lungs and heart, Hoolow busied himself with gathering materials for a fire. Squatting, he pinioned a dry stick between his feet and spun another between the flats of his hands. A tendril of smoke ascended from the point of friction. Its scent provoked another hunter to fling himself from the carcass, his cheek to the ground to blow from just the right angle, his bloody arms held back along his sides to avoid dampening the tinder. A tiny flame appeared, and Hoolow stopped his drilling and fed it dry grass until it soared. He piled on the sticks and branches he'd gathered. He was the youngest hunter. For his effort, the graybeard tore him a piece of lung, its spongy flesh saturated with blood. Hoolow sucked and chewed. Along with the others, he became absorbed in feasting.

They hastily attempted to drink up all the blood before it drenched into the dirt. It contained the animal's life force, and thus, divided between the hunters, the bull's individual power dispersed into their blood. They felt it pounding, surging through their vessels—their special reward for a successful hunt. Each tasted from the green fermenting vat of stomach, grimacing at its acidity. They roasted the organ meats over the fire, reserving a few precious morsels for particular friends. Seeing them being squirreled away by the others, Hoolow forgot his inhibition and collected his own share; he thought of the girl. The hunters became giddy, relishing at the same time complaining as they compared their distended bellies. They laughed, and the tears squeezed out, even from Hoolow's eyes. They saved the bladder for the children.

Gorged, they lolled about the fire, winking off into brief sleeps until the graybeard hauled himself toward the empty carcass and began pulling at its skin. The others joined him, using their stones to shear the filaments that attached the flesh. The empty carcass, although still weighted by bones and muscle, moved more easily. They manipulated it until it lay naked and pink, save the head, whose clouded eyes looked on dolefully. It took all of their hands to spread open the heavy skin upon the ground. It was of a piece in the shape of the animal lying splayed upon its belly except for the gaping tear in the rump, where the graybeard's spear had glanced after the first thrust, and two neat holes in the neck that could be stitched with sinew. The graybeard knelt and arranged the flap so that its seam matched with the rest of the skin. He fingered the grass blades that poked through the narrow opening and hooed. He felt strength surge through him.

Next they worked through the muscles, scraping their stones down the long bones, the tender fresh meat falling in hunks. Despite their fullness, they cut mouthfuls when they came upon white deposits of fat. They smiled and hummed as they worked.

At dusk they sat around the fire, pounding the bones. The task absorbed them: the sound of breaking, the screech as they twisted to release the marrow. The taste was round and mellow, but with their bellies achingly full, it mattered little. They ate to avoid waste, to avoid having to carry the heavy bones back to camp. They aligned their bones on their anvil stones and pounded them with the granite cobbles that lay about. Pound, crack, screech. Together they fell into a rhythm, the bones chanting, "Eat, eat, eat." The graybeard began to hoo a melody. The others joined him, even Hoolow, entranced as he was by the breaking of bones and forced feeding. He fell in with the wordless song, so that it seemed the bones broke themselves. He watched his hands do the work and swallowed mouthfuls during pauses, without disturbing the melody that crooned out of him unbidden. Suddenly, the graybeard jumped to his feet. He supported his protruding belly with a hand on either side. He hopped on one foot, then the other. He flopped his head back and howled. The other hunters joined him in circumnavigating the fire, supporting their bellies. The graybeard slapped his hands down his sides. He shuffled his feet. Those in line behind him copied his dance. Already intoxicated with animal fat, it wasn't long before they tipped and rolled with dizziness. They fell to the ground with eyes squeezed shut against the entoptic images that coalesced to reenact the hunt. On hands and knees they scrambled and barked. They tore at the bull with their long prognathous jaws, their ears laid back. Hoolow participated in the frenzy, caught up in their collective play, yet subtly aware that he did not see as they saw.

Despite their long evening revelry, they woke at the first light. Before leaving the carcass, the stones asked to be released from their shafts, "Let the stones stay here to mingle with the bones of the newest brother. The work is done." The hunters unwound the twine, careful not to splinter the shaft ends, who remained loyal to the tribe, except for the one belonging to the young hunter, whose shaft had been snapped by the shoulder of the bull. It also asked to be left with the carcass, saying, "Let this one stay here. It is tired." The young hunter laid it within the ribs of the bull and stood for a moment looking down on it. Where it was oiled smooth by his grip, it gleamed. It glowed with his essence. He rolled up the new stiffening hide for consolation and tucked it under his arm. It sagged burdensomely, but pride kept his muscles from cramping. The discarded spear sang a keening song as they slung their heavy sacks and headed toward their shelter and the rest of the tribe, for once taking the shortest path, as the groaning meat meant to attract stalkers. The men steadied their loads with one hand where it sliced at their shoulders. With their right hands, they hefted their empty spears and let them slide through their fingers so the butts pounded the ground in counterpoint to their footfalls, the rhythmic beats doubling their number to the ears of potential predators. None approached, and they proceeded safely. The sacks of meat slapped their backs.

In the shelter the first woman awoke with the dream of their hunters' return. She shook awake the one lying next to her, who opened her eyes to the staring inquiry of the first, their noses touching in the still dim light. Their mutual smiles affirmed the collectivity of the dream. The heads of the others popped up one by one, each glancing to the rest to confer her premonition. They celebrated in nonsensical chatter. Ignoring the cascade of nuts, they stoked the fire high for the meat they knew was coming. An old one shouted, "Quiet! Listen." All fell silent, but hearing no telltale sign of the hunters' approach, they resumed their tasks, more quietly at first, but soon growing in volume as they were invigorated by lust for the succulent meat.

The children stood facing out along the ledge, chewing their fists in anticipation. They spotted the hunters and, running out to greet them, were rewarded with the inflated bladder. When the women reached them, they grabbed at the bulging sacks of meat before remembering to caress them everywhere. The men laughed and, massaging their distended bellies, shooed them back toward the shelter. Wide-eyed, the children patted the hunters' bellies like drums, dipping their digits into the hollow buttons when it was not their turn to kick the bladder and scream after it as it bounded over the ground. The men joined them in their play, occasionally stooping to upend a little runner and spin her around with feet kicking skyward. They continued until an inadvertently placed foot flattened the bladder with a flatulent bleat. All play suspended, and those children who were in the midst of being hoisted were lowered before they all burst out with laughter and mock farts. It was only then that the children were captivated by the wafts of roasting meat. They marched back to the shelter trailed by the hunters, who relished the scene of the women blowing on the sizzling strips of flesh, yet still managing to burn their lips with eagerness. The hunters relaxed as they watched the children clamor for and receive their portions. They took their time in presenting the small tidbits they'd secreted away.

Hoolow didn't wait for the girl to finish her meat before he grabbed her fat-slicked fingers. They slid through his grip, and she stumbled as he tried to pull her to standing and that made them both laugh. They hardly noticed the children following them as they hurried toward the near bushes. There was no need to concentrate; the girl drew every dram of his attention, leaving nothing for the generation of thoughts until, lying spent, the rustle of leaves moved by stifled breath ignited a whirl of anger in him. Indignant at having been observed in a sacred act, he leapt to his feet and shouted at the children, waving his fists above their heads. They scattered in a gale of giggles quickly gobbled by darkness. Without their little forms at which to direct his anger, humiliation hung on him. He tried to beat it back with his fists pumping the air, but his effort garnered another spate of giggles, this one emanating from the girl, who still reclined beautifully. He dropped his arms and turned to look down on her; the sight of her body glowing in starlight drained him of evil emotion and filled him with warmth, secure in their mutual love. For a moment no other member of the tribe existed, and then their pounding footfalls called out across the plain; he and the girl could not help but reply.

Racing back to the shelter, they took up their positions in line with the others, whose rows moved in waves, each party stepping forward and stamping first right, then left and back, causing a ripple that zigzagged through every member of the tribe, children and old participating with equal relish. Handclaps provided a second rhythmic line punctuated by modulated hoos. The graybeard broke away and danced around the fire, hefting his imaginary spear high so all could see it flash like a blue lightning bolt. He let it fly with a mighty death cry. The young hunter quit ranks and danced with his feet alarmingly close to the fire. He rapidly sucked air in and out of his open mouth, puffing his cheeks and snapping his belly until the muscles of his abdomen seized and contracted, drawing him into a crouch. He shambled about the fire, face to the ground, allowing his arms to swing side to side. The tribe, seeing his transformation, increased their rhythm. The graybeard led the first row to circle the fire, and the others fell in, spiraling around as the young hunter swayed ever closer to the flames, only retreating when he singed the sides of his feet. The people grew more excited. Their anticipation wound them to ever greater pitch. Finally, the young hunter stumbled and allowed himself to roll over the flames that bounced him to solid ground. He turned over twice before stopping against their dancing shins. The women fell on him, arranging his limbs and supporting his head with their hands. They turned his neck so the trance-blood leaking from his nose could dribble to the dust thus consecrating their shelter. They massaged his cold hands and feet and palpated his lifeless biceps, while the graybeard took over his role. When the trance-blood filled his nasal passages, he huffed through his nostrils, expelling an impressive spray. Upon seeing it, the rest of the tribe screeched, many falling to the ground, while the rest increased the pace of their dancing to a frenzy. Unimpeded by the crowd, they circled tight around the fire, stepping over their trance-limp fellows where necessary. Hoolow was among them, dancing in the mystery. In the morning he would listen to the stories of trance visions with wonder, but now every thought was obliterated by the rhythmically stamping feet. Their sound reverberated through the shelter, their action driving a groove into the hard-packed dirt until exhaustion overtook them. One by one they fell amongst the writhing trancers and slept through dreams of astonishing color. Hoolow was the last to feel the earth. He closed his eyes to a vision of the girl.

A globe of light encased her as she moved through the dim shelter. He was a shadow, observing, nearly dissipated by her emanation. She filled her sling with nuts from the back of the shelter and carried them to the simmering firepit, where she placed them amongst the embers. Hoolow admired the peak of her cheekbone in profile and the black tip of her eyelash projecting past the translucent wedge of her eye. His throat tightened as the young hunter approached, his body shining with fresh sweat and a smear of dried blood encrusting his upper lip. His expression was a perfect post-trance blend of confidence and vulnerability, beautiful even to Hoolow, who felt his heart lose its mooring in his chest. It rebounded as the girl turned from the young hunter, whose surprise Hoolow had no time to relish, rapt as he was by her legs ratcheting her up from her squat by the fire. He watched her come to him, stepping over the sleeping bodies of her mother and sister on her journey, her brilliant eyes trained on him. She folded herself down beside him, fitting her body to his like another limb. Their bones rocked into place, and he watched her smiling until he awoke.

The women and children had gone on their rounds, but the other hunters slept, exhausted by their consecutive nights of dancing and visions. Hoolow scratched his belly. Having woken naturally, he remembered his dream. He touched his flaccid genitals, surprised by their state, but then remembered his real encounter with the girl. He sniffed his hand, bringing the full picture of her, carried on her lingering scent, into focus.

He picked the few discarded nuts from the fire and walked to the spring, where he bathed himself, finally, luxuriating in the water, floating on his back, looking up and seeing nothing but the smooth even blue that soothed as he reviewed the anxieties he'd felt with his fellow hunters. The water lapping along his side rocked away every prior feeling of discomfort. He allowed his lower half to sink, bringing him to vertical, and from this vantage he saw the children huddled behind a bush near the shore. Stealthily he stroked to the edge of the spring and, drawing himself out, crept up to join them, remembering his own childhood playfulness and feeling a bit ashamed of his earlier outburst. He thought to himself, it would not be an unpleasant vision, and he couldn't deny his curiosity. But the joyous vision he spied through a fork of twigs was the most unpleasant of his young life. There the girl straddled the young hunter with her face beaming skyward in ecstasy. She squeaked as the hunter lifted her hips with his rhythmic thrusts, and Hoolow reeled back, losing his footing. A slender stick beneath his buttocks emitted a loud crack that made the children turn and laugh, and even more horrifying—the girl and the hunter emerged from behind the bush. Looking up, Hoolow's eyes fastened to the hunter's glistening tumescence. He clawed himself to his feet and ran but not fast enough to escape the high tinkling laughter of the girl backed by deeper guffaws.

When he was out of breath, he went to his knees and covered his eyes. Through the darkness of his hands the scene glowed, its colors vibrant like the ones he'd shared with his tribemates before the death of his mother but from which he'd become estranged. He threw open his hands, hoping the light would dissipate the awful sight, and discovered himself in a valley whose opposing hillsides were stacked with basalt blocks that had been propelled into place by a massive explosion in a prior epoch; Hoolow felt the aftershocks in his chest. They reverberated through the superimposed image of the girl's arching back, vibrating her to further heights of ecstasy. He squeezed his eyes shut and tried to shake the image away, but she only trembled. How could she? The brutality of her act was incomprehensible and its afterimage apparently indelible. Once again, the elusiveness of the visions seemed heartrendingly proportionate to his desire to see them, of their usefulness to him. It was the girl who had come to him like a cure. When his thoughts became too much to bear, or his knowledge of his remoteness from the visions of the others too killing, then there she would be, offering her body as his sanctuary. She had no need of sanctuary as she was like all the others, seeing as they saw. There was nothing mutual between them. His illusion shattered.

He stretched himself on the dirt and struggled to keep his thoughts at bay. Despair expanded into the vacuum. At midday he shielded his eyes from the black birds that wheeled overhead. He turned his cheek to the dirt and left it thus for so long that the pebbles therein left pock marks. As night fell he considered lying still and waiting for whatever beast would come to consume him, but he pulled himself up and staggered toward the shelter, dehydrated and weary.

As Hoolow approached, he could see the young hunter standing with his back to the ledge and the others arrayed in front of him, their rapt faces illuminated by firelight. He seemed to be acting a strange part. He hugged his arms tight across his body and looking down, aimlessly shuffled his feet. It resembled no animal Hoolow could think of. He drew closer, full of interest despite himself. The young hunter dropped his arms and stared up at the ceiling as if it were sky. He staggered a few dreamy steps. The rest of the tribe laughed, and Hoolow got an inkling of what the play was about. The hunter's next act confirmed it: he was suddenly angry for no apparent reason. He stamped his foot and flailed his arms. The rest of the tribe exploded into hysterics of laughter, not least of all because one of the women had spotted Hoolow and pointed him out to the others. His stricken form went unnoticed by the young hunter, who continued his act, kicking the dust as if it had affronted him and for his finale—stubbing his toe and hopping on one foot while managing to look both pained and confused, a perfect imitation of the expression all in the tribe associated with Hoolow. The young hunter dropped his act to join in the laughter, and as he did, he noticed the one not laughing. Hoolow stood to the side, wearing the very expression he'd just seen mocked, and the congruity provoked further gales of mirth. The young hunter went to him with tears on his cheeks and his arm extended to clap his back, but Hoolow hit it away. As if witnessing an unexpected third act, the tribe fell silent and watched Hoolow push his way to the back of the shelter, where he threw himself down against the wall. He huddled into a tight ball and ducked his head away from their view. They shifted their attention from him to the young hunter, who was as confused as they were. He gave his shoulders an exaggerated shrug, eliciting a few chuckles, but the mood was dampened.

The graybeard stepped forward to help the women prepare the fire for cooking. Hoolow was unmoved by the resultant aromas. His body remained tense long after the others had started snoring. Finally he fell to a fitful sleep.

When the other hunters tried to rouse him for their party, he beat them away, and they went off chuckling. After their departure and that of the women, he lay in his depression, determined to get the sleep his humiliation had denied him earlier, but the emptiness of the shelter called out for thoughts of the girl. He couldn't prevent the thoughts from pouring through, maddening him. He needed to see her, to know if she was with the hunter or the other women. He arose, and without even inspecting the fire for leftover nuts, he stalked the girl as if she were prey. With his head swimming over remembrances of the horror and pain she'd caused him, the color of her scent faded in and out. The surprising strength of the other hunters confused him. The astringent smell of well steeped human flesh burned yellow in his nostrils. He pricked his ears, and indeed he could hear the purple footfalls of a party of hunters moving through the tall grass. He retreated behind a boulder and hoped his own scent trail was not so strong. Luckily their accumulated scent preceded them. They passed him by with eyes focused for signs of their prey in the grass stretched before them. He watched the retreat of their bare buttocks bunching and smoothing in time to their quick synchronized steps. He watched until the grass closed around them and only their heads bobbed distantly, their spear points at perfect, unwavering angles. He was alone again.

He heard their easy laughter up ahead and concealed himself in his approach. The women clustered within talking distance of one another. Hunkered on haunches, they used their digging sticks to dislodge the deep tubers, brushing them free of dirt with their hands before laying them in their slings like insensible infants, while their real children chased each other through the grass, pausing to investigate all the interesting bugs who didn't flee upon inspection. Hoolow scanned their faces, looking for the girl, finding her with her sling only half full and lying spilling to the side as she braided her little sister's tresses. He swallowed, hungry for her at the same time appalled by the beauty of her fingers delicately performing the plaits. Their gentility was at odds with what he knew to be her malicious character. He couldn't help but wonder what her reaction to seeing him would be. Made dizzy by his conflicted feelings, he stumbled from his hiding place, revealing himself to the girl as well as the other women. All the easy, chatting activity stopped as the women and children turned to look at the man in their midst. No man had ever dared join them while they engaged in this activity and yet here he was, not much beyond boyhood. Had he forgotten he was a man? A frisson of fear and suspicion tingled through the females. His presence violated them in some manner that was impossible to articulate, yet each felt the unease acutely. They did not think of the meaning behind his presence, only its oddness, but one who remembered his mother well, spoke to diffuse the tension of the novel situation. "Maybe that's an old one," she said slyly, as an old and frail male sometimes won the privilege of traveling with the women.

Catching on to the joke, her friend picked it up, chiding, "That one hasn't a hair on the fruit, not even a man yet." She pointed to Hoolow's genitals, and he moved a hand to cover them. Seeing his embarrassment, they all laughed, convinced of his harmlessness. They'd come to expect confusion from Hoolow. Only he would think to do something no other man would dare, but he did it without guile.

Sparked by the new levity he'd brought to their situation, the girl skipped to his side, grinning seductively. The other women watched astonished as Hoolow folded his arms over his chest and glared at her. The girl only laughed harder, assuming it a part of his ploy. She pulled at his forearm, but he squeezed it tighter and swiveled his shoulders to shake off her grip. Surprised by his inscrutability, she ran back to the other women, who were holding their bellies with laughter. "Maybe it's an old one after all," said her mother, wiping her tears with her thumb. Hoolow walked back along the path with their laughter chasing him, but he did not allow himself to run.

In his petulance, he came upon the bladder lying in the grass, busted and filled with ants. He thought, what had it been for? A few moments of laughing and playing, the particulars of which were now forgotten by all who had participated, himself included. And how was the whole of life any different from being batted around like a bladder to end up broken and consumed by ants in the dirt? He kicked it, but retaining none of its once happy buoyancy, it flopped back to earth a short distance away, the ants still clinging.

He ambled down to the spring and searched the shore for flat pebbles he could skip across the surface, a game he remembered playing as a child. He skipped pebbles, one skip, two. One pebble skipped three times, beyond which there was no counting, only many. Few stones skipped many times, but when his next toss accomplished the feat it hardly caused a blip in his sour mood. He flung the stones as if flaying the surface of the spring from its living depths. It was mysterious and dark down there. He remembered swimming as a child with his eyes open despite the stinging mud, desperate to see through the green murk, but only able to make out vague shapes and snatches of movement. His life on land was not much different. He couldn't see what the others saw or he could sort of see, but it was murky. He imagined that he saw, that's what it was. But perhaps they did not really see either. They were all in on the secret seeing, pretending so as to fool him into thinking he was freakish, half-blind. Or if they did see everything all alike, wasn't that evidence of his own superiority? He alone among them had a distinguishing vision. He discriminated in what he saw. It was not an unfiltered feed from one body to the next. He picked up another stone, pitched it and watched it skip—one, two, three—then sink below the surface. He searched the bank for another suitable stone. He picked up one that wasn't flat enough and tried it anyway. It plopped and sunk. Hoolow watched its wake of concentric ripples expand—one, two, three—he turned and kicked a stone that rested too high above the others. He laid a hand against the back of his neck and felt where it had grown too hot from the sun. He headed toward the cool shade of the shelter and rested there, thankful to be alone.

This time when the hunters and the women returned they avoided him. He thought he identified a few wary looks cast his way and was happy for it, thinking, that's right, fear Hoolow, you thought-less animals. But as they settled down, his hunger drew him into their midst, and they did not deny him the food he'd done nothing to help procure. He ate with shame and paid close attention during the singing, hitting all the right notes while avoiding sight of the girl; he edited her voice out of the chorus sounding in his ears, and for awhile he was free from thoughts.

That night in sleep he came upon a lion and was at first startled, heart pounding, body tensed in anticipation of attack, but the big cat was preoccupied with consuming its recent prey. Hoolow's eyes fell to the bloody carcass held between its paws while it gnawed a limb. There he saw the unblemished remnants of a hairless brown skin. No longer fearing for his life, he allowed his eyes to trail down a lower appendage to where it ended in a perfectly formed foot, its unmistakable arch turned in his direction. He couldn't help but smile. Satisfaction swelled in him as if it were his own belly filling—up, up, up—the nourishment spreading to his fingertips. He woke with his back angled painfully against a depression in the hard-packed floor, but it wasn't enough to obliterate the sense of satisfaction fostered by the dream. He rubbed his eyes and blinked around the shelter at the long gray shadows of morning. All of the people were gone. The other hunters had not tried to wake him before setting off. Good. They'd finally given up on him, and his life would be easier from now on. He crawled to the fire and picked the remaining nuts from amongst the smoldering embers. There were a few discarded greens as well. He thought of finding the women. Then he would see the girl and maybe kill her. Should a creature that inflicted so much pain be allowed to live? If only he could be assured that his dream would come true. If his earlier dream was any indication, then the opposite would happen, and he could expect to see her slay a lion with her bare hands.

Hoolow had to cross a greater distance than the day before and cursed over the women's calloused footprints. All of their gathering could be accomplished closer to camp; they were going to play. He thought they meant to tease him, make him work for their company, but when he burst into their midst, they seemed as surprised as on the previous day.

They looked up from the sensuous designs they were spreading with their fingertips, their ankles sunk deep in the clay. The women had traveled far to find the deposits of white clay, and they wouldn't allow Hoolow's presence to dampen their joy. They continued to reach below the surface for cool handfuls they massaged between their fingers and used to draw intricate stripes over each other's bodies, outlining the curves, spiraling in to the important creases. They used it to sculpt their hair, stood back and hooted at their handiwork.

Shocked by their altered appearances, Hoolow stood agog at the beauty of the lines curving over their bodies, drawing his eyes in circles over their hips.

The girl ran to his side and playfully swiped at him with her clay-covered fingers, but he pulled away so that she caught only his forearm with four stripes. He hurried to smear it against his side, not wanting her to have the satisfaction of marking him. He scowled at her. He watched her face fall, thinking he'd made himself known to her; now he could reach out his hands, close them around her throat and seal this moment of her realization of his hatred in both their memories. She turned. There was still time to pounce upon her back, knock her to the ground with the weight of his body and pummel her head. But his eyes fell to her pretty ankles, so delicate he could barely comprehend how she walked.

He ran. He tripped and scraped blood from his knees. His hands flew to his aching side and encountered the smear of white clay. It crumbled from his skin at his touch, and he pressed it with his palm, trying to mold it back into place with his sweat. He wept. If only he'd had the courage to kill her, then he would be free now and not this pitiful wreck, clinging to a scrap of clay. He rolled in the dirt, sobbing. What he needed was banishment. Why hadn't the people enforced his banishment long ago? If his difference was this obvious to himself, then it must be equally so to them, and of course, it was true. Their looks of confusion were a daily reinforcement of his oddness, but they seemed not to grasp the depth of it. How could they? It was intolerable. He could no longer watch them carrying on around him as if he had no more thoughts than they did. He must escape. If they were too simple to banish him, then he would do it himself.

He stood, squared his shoulders and squeezed his fists by his sides. He chose a direction and walked, then turned back.

The girl may be as the rest, a stupid creature with whom he had no hope of meaningful connection, but all the same, he required a last look. He could do it without being seen. He must not be seen and looked upon with pity or confusion or whatever other misguided emotion she had ready for him. The sun was past the middle of the sky, so the women must be on their way back to the shelter. If he was quick, he might intercept them en route, view them from behind a rock, invisible, and then he could leave forever, find a place for himself alone. He could not think beyond finding such a place.

It was well past midday when he'd nearly reached the shelter without sight of the women. He figured they'd have returned along this route earlier, but probably they lingered over their silly play in the mud. He settled himself behind a rock and waited. They'd be along soon. The sun moved across the sky, and he began sweating sitting still. He grew parched. Could he risk a walk to the spring? He peeked around the rock and looking in every direction, saw no one. Where were the women? He knew the route they would have taken, and they should have passed by here already. He stood up but did not walk toward the spring. Instead he backtracked along the women's usual route, not the secret one, but the one everyone used when in a hurry to get back to the camp before dark, as they must be hurrying now. He walked far to the side of the path, going from rock to bush and only just keeping the path in sight, still not wishing to be seen. Finally he heard the women wailing up ahead. He crouched low in the tall grass and crept up to where he could see them gathered near a rock overhang. The girl's mother was at the center of the group. She wailed the loudest, and the others took turns stroking her. Hoolow circled around to where he could climb the rocks and have a look down on the scene. He had little worry of being seen in this endeavor; the women were preoccupied by some dreadful occurrence. The blood thrummed in his ears as he climbed hand over hand, his toes blindly finding the crevices he needed to push off from. At the top he encountered the fresh scat of a large cat. Its animal stink menaced the entire area. Hoolow lowered himself to his belly and slithered to the edge. He hung his head over, just as the cat must have done. He knew what he would see, the twisted body of the girl lying at the center of the clutch of mourning women; those on the periphery screeched and beat the ground. Her mother and little sister beseeched her to get up. They pulled at her limbs and cried louder when they fell back, limp as the rest of her sprawling lifelessness, bending the pliant grass that sprang back around her. He watched from above, thoughts racing through his mind—would a warning have made any difference? Would they have stopped their play earlier and hurried to get back to the shelter before the attack could take place? If he had told. But he had thought his dreams meant nothing.

As night fell, they moved off. Hoolow scrambled down to follow them, unworried about being seen. The women were too busy supporting the grieving mother, occasionally having to restrain her from turning back, her younger daughter clinging, sobbing, to her thigh. They were easy to see in the darkness. With their white paint glowing, they could be the animals without bodies, only liquid bones that swirled as they walked. Hoolow followed, mesmerized by their flowing bones. Silently, he threatened the predators he suspected of lurking in the pitch black shadows. Should the lion reappear he'd throw himself to the ground in front of it, offer it his throat. In fact he longed for the opportunity to make this sacrifice. He crouched behind the same rock where he had waited through the afternoon, and watched the women proceed to the shelter, where the men had stoked the fire to a roaring beacon. The girl's mother calmed. The men came down and surrounded her. The graybeard lifted the little sister and tucked her head to the crook of his neck. Hoolow could see his silver chin hairs reflecting the light of the fire. The night filled with voices as the women told their story. The men fell silent with grief, and Hoolow watched from behind the rock.

The fire was allowed to die down and with it faded Hoolow's last glimpse of the tribe. He imagined them offering the girl's mother and sister the tenderest pieces of meat. He saw them sitting by the fire, morose, being petted and soothed by the others, as he could hear voices singing, hoo loo, hoo, like the sound of his own name, but he couldn't make out the voice of the mother. Her remaining daughter would be sitting in her lap, perhaps reaching up to push pieces of succulent meat between her mother's lips. The girl would have done this. If she were alive she would have expressed her compassion in just that way. The perfect configuration of her face wavered in his mind, but he felt her innocent love as boundless, enveloping, and knew that he was the one who was petty and small.

He returned to where her body lay in disarray, every curve accentuated with white streaks of clay. He chased off the dogs that would tear her apart and picked up her body, already cool and rigid. He carried it until his knees shook and his arms were weak. He lowered her to the ground and with his fingers carved a round depression in the earth like the ones midwives carved beneath delivering mothers. He struggled to bend her limbs to the appropriate shape, but her body had stiffened. Although he felt deserving of this demonstration of her disdain, he realized it was not her will that resisted him. He sat next to her body and pulled at the dry weeds. He twisted them, rolling the ends between his finger and thumb until they made a chain, a twine like the ones the hunters used to attach their spear points, something he'd never been able to do when he'd tried. He recalled how his ineptitude had made the others laugh but felt more shame at his reaction. His anger now seemed useless, a stupid indulgence that not only rendered him undeserving of their affection but unable to reciprocate. When the twine had grown long enough, he held her knees between his own and bore down on her with his chest, using his full weight of which he'd been so careful during sex; he bound her knees to her chest, folding her elbows down into her belly. He rubbed her body with the red earth and covered her with stones, because he couldn't bear the thought of her beautiful body disarticulated by the animals slavering to eat her.

As he lifted each new rock to the pile, remembered feelings of love washed through him. The magic of being lost in her superseded all of the rage and hurt that her subsequent action elicited, leaving him so weak that he sat by the cairn to review the moments of his consuming infatuation. He had been assailed by thoughts, and then she was there, her aura offering a bubble of peace. His thoughts were subsumed in what he assumed was their mutual feeling. But now he knew there was nothing in her that knew how to love the way that he did. There was no selfishness and no need for possession. She was as all the others in the purity and breadth of her feeling, and he was unworthy of its compass. He thought of the others back at the shelter—her mother and little sister, the graybeard, the young hunter and the other young hunters who were his brothers, although so different from him—all singing a singular song, and he imagined each one falling individually to the earth, where they squirmed for a moment before lying still with death, alone. The others would not be there then. They might mourn for a day or several, but they had no need of the one; they would go on being the tribe the same as ever, but he was one. Alone.

He began his journey into the night.

PART TWO

HOOLOW'S MOTHER WAS taller than the other women. Her hair was the longest. She wore it in a great pile of plaits, and the other women vied to coif her. Sometimes they worked on her two at a time, while she reclined with her neck propped on a rock and Hoolow hopping back and forth over the smooth dome of her belly. She reached to tickle his feet in mid-flight. Everyone had thought he would be her last.

The hunter who was her favorite had a beard that was still black. She doted on him, and he advocated the validity of her hunt dreams to the men, for she didn't dream like the other women alone, but as the women and men combined. She dreamed the fields and all the plants they contained; into them she herded every manner of beast and was able to spot the weakest based upon what they ate, because she knew the right victual for every ailment. As she told her dreams, images blossomed behind Hoolow's eyes. He sat as rapt as the others while she intoned.

The older boys, some of them his brothers, tolerated him, often treating him as a plaything, which made him happy despite his frequent role as a prey animal they practiced jabbing with sticks, only choosing ones that broke easily against his skin lest they leave a mark and incur the wrath of his powerful mother. She had reached the point of teetering when she walked, and it was too soon for that, but her hips, having been opened by many prior births, were loose, causing an oscillation in her walk that swayed first side to side, then front to back as her belly pulled her forward and she lifted it, but her shoulders stayed straight, her head erect on her slender neck.

As they made their way back to the shelter with their collected bounty, his mother's voice was the loudest. She sang out above the rest as she walked in front, and the others did their best to imitate her quality. Her belly caused her to lose her balance and slide over the loose rocks of the embankment they'd built to dam the spring. A crack caught her ankle before she had a chance to land in a violent heap. Because there was no scream, everyone heard the spalling snap of her lower leg. The fine splinters of bone spiraled into her firm calf muscle, and it was already swelling before the others could reach her. Hoolow was the first at her side. She untwisted her body and ran her hands over her belly before looking up at him. She drew a hand tenderly across his cheek and tweaked his quivering chin before the other women surrounded her, pushing him out of her reach. They fussed in moving more rocks than necessary to free her. The ones who could find no more room on her body to place a hand, busied themselves with clearing a path in front of her and her supporters, all the way to the top of the embankment. They flitted about the slow moving huddle, shoving the children ahead. A few of them ran, but Hoolow hung back, stunned. They were still a good distance from the shelter when the men came running, the blackbeard in front. He pushed through the crowd and bent deeply to lift the heavy woman She groaned then, but it was at the uncomfortable pressure of her belly and not the leg that was already swollen stiff and numb. The women still tried to help, supporting her legs and her crown of hair. She smiled and laid her head against the blackbeard's shoulder. She remained still in his arms even to the last of his shuddering steps before he placed her in the deep depression she'd dug especial at the back of the shelter. It was big enough for her belly and Hoolow both. The blackbeard laid against her back.

At first they cared for her, and she helped them by telling which plants to bring. She smiled and relaxed while they chewed poultices with which to plaster her useless limb. They fought to arrange her hair, but as the smell grew worse, the competition fell off. They scrunched up their faces and turned their heads away.

When they passed close by, they pinched their noses and made their mouths grim. They brushed their hands beneath their nostrils, saying, "One forgot to go outside to defecate."

Only Hoolow was ever by her side, listening to the snide comments spoken loudly from the opposite end of the shelter. He could see the word they were hiding behind their grimaces—death. Death. Death was what they smelled, and Hoolow smelled it too, but while they were too afraid to come close, he was too afraid to move away.

When the fever came, even the blackbeard kept his distance. The terrorized tribe stared across the empty depressions at Hoolow's attempts to push food between her lips, but she squeezed them tight, as well as her eyes, and there was nothing he could do other than consume her portion. In the morning her place was empty; his side where she had lain was as cold as the other.

With Hoolow still confused, they gathered their few belongings and abandoned their dwelling. Their brief period of ministration now served them for mourning, and relief supplanted any grief. There was only Hoolow's tearful following to contend with. There was no lack of compassion on his behalf. Many wanted to go to him, for his cries penetrated their eyes despite their unwillingness to look down at his contorted face. They jerked their children closer and walked on. Hoolow pursued, pulling on their hands where they were allowed to dangle. Soon the entire tribe walked holding their elbows, staring straight ahead.

They built a fire on the open plain under a clear sky. Hoolow's eyes were dry. He watched solemnly, as if finally accepting his place on the periphery. He made no attempt to move closer, only stared at the leaping orange flame from a distance, and there were no other colors dancing. His vision had become stark, the colors for ever after an occasional occurrence, appearing only when he was not distracted by thoughts.

Across the flames the blackbeard watched him. He saw his face become calm, resolute; in its expression resided the most remarkable resemblance to his mother, and yet it was tempered by something even more familiar. Hoolow's body glowed fiercely with the color of the tribe. His vigor had not waned during the long march, and the blackbeard could see his hunger spark at the sight of the meat scraps the women now held over the flames.

The blackbeard went to him smiling and laughed at his suspicious look. He hooked his hands into his armpits and hoisted him. Hoolow felt himself released from the tired hold of the earth. He flew, and a laugh of pure glee leaped from his lungs. Alive again, he sat with the others, close against the side of the blackbeard, who took occasion to pat his shoulders.

He sucked at a piece of dry meat, while the women stroked him and wiped the bramble cuts on his ankles with their saliva as if he had always been their own and they'd never intended to leave him behind nor feared his contamination.

A death had first defined him and now another propelled him to this new destiny, perhaps the one he should have chosen at the first, for what if his mother lived as other than a voice in his memory? But no, everyone knew separation from the tribe meant death. There had been no searching and never any expectation of return.

He stopped, for the sound of his footfalls prevented the clear recollection of his mother's voice. He remained motionless, focused, but all she said was, "Don't eat." The plant at his feet was a hoary weed, barely distinguishable from those on either side of it. The plant had no voice, nor did his mother. She was dead, and he realized the sound he heard was generated from some undefined thing inside of him, but there was no doubting its feminine timbre, and wasn't it just like the women to monopolize the food when it was not their right to do so? As a child he'd picked and eaten all the plants he'd craved, and now he craved a new one.

It tasted bitter, and his first instinct was to spit and desist, but in his ire—against the women, his kind, his lowly self—the bitterness seemed appropriate. He chewed and swallowed, his mouth salivating mightily over the dry weed. It nettled his throat all the way down and made his stomach bubble upon impact, but he continued chewing until the contraction of his belly drew him forward. He faced the earth with foam leaking from his lips. He dropped the weed and clutched his cramping abdomen. Allowing his knees to buckle, he reached one hand toward the ground to steady his descent until his full body twisted in the dirt, and he thought, good. Good. It will be over, finally. The women will have their revenge, the girl, all of them. If the men could see, they would clutch their bellies and writhe in mockery. Little ridges of dirt rose around his uncontrolled gesticulations. From the corners of his eyes, he saw them like mountains growing up around him as he was sinking down. Down in the earth, where these towers of dirt would collapse over him, sealing him in. His neck flung his head from side to side, and his belly contracted further, jerking his nose to his knees as he continued to fall. Deeper into the earth. The light above receded. Tendrils of dirt trickled down in colored beads, joining together in segmented threads that helixed in their descent. The walls around him revolved and became segmented by panels of colors that swirled and blurred the images who observed his falling. He felt his body shrinking, arms and legs retracting into his torso and his skin toughening to carapace. His neck pulled his head into his body until his eyes looked out from his shoulders and he walked with his chin flush with his belly, nearly touching the ground. Three pairs of legs propelled him through the underground tunnel as if he'd been a termite his entire life. The winding tunnel opened into a chamber, its walls and ceiling scraped smooth by thousands of feet, the floor crowded with eggs. He tended the eggs as if he were himself their mother, filled with natural feeling, his whole self imbued by the pleasure of nurturing. He rotated the eggs between his feather-like limbs; they glided in their gelatinous sheathes. In the next compartment the larva squirmed en mass, and he scurried over their bodies with no fear of harming, regurgitating into every mouth that tickled his chin with upward stretching mandibles. When he was empty, he followed his fellow nursemales through another tunnel; it opened onto the chamber where the queen resided with her great pulsating abdomen of rainbow colors and her scissor-like jaws moving up and down and left to right as she gnawed through the bodies of the males lined up before her. Within the confines of the tunnel, he struggled to rotate his body. As his foremost feet scrabbled over the wall, they fell into the opening of a tributary passageway. He scurried into it and ascended through its spirals. A tiny light appeared above him. He crawled toward it at full speed only to discover that the passage linked to an aperture on a sheer cliff of dirt. Granules of the lip gave way beneath his feet, and he felt himself falling once again. The two plates on his back spread apart, and gossamer wings emerged to lift him, legs dangling, stunned as he watched the ground retreat in fits. His wings stirred up turbulence as he bumbled horizontally, the air rushing over him in a euphoric wave that caused his wings to stretch to the sides, stimulating their growth. They spread out with feathers that encroached onto his thorax. The chitin split apart at his belly and migrated over his sides to knot into the flexible vertebrae that allowed him to soar high and far. He looked down on an expanse of rippling blue water like he'd never seen before. A flicker beneath the waves caught his attention, and before any thought could assail him, he drew his wings in tight and angled his head down for the plunge. His long pointed bill split the surface of the water, and he felt it envelop him. He paddled his feet, driving himself deeper, flashes of silver all around him. They turned in unison and back again in their original direction like the leaves on a cedar. These synchronized movements entranced. His feathers fused to translucent shingles. His head narrowed, squeezing out any thought trying to materialize, and he joined in the dance, flashing one direction, then the other. He breathed the water like a warm soup washing over his gills and then spilling over the silently snapping sinew of his body. It moved to the dance in the even blue, whose salt sloughed his consciousness in microscopic bits that drifted down, down, down.

He woke in the cave with no recollection of his physical journey, more surprised by the restoration of his body than by its unexplained displacement. He turned his head to see the opening hung with the gray sheen of moonlight. His knees trembled as he got to his feet and waved an outstretched hand to find the wall of the cave, which he used to help guide him over the uneven floor to the mouth. He looked out over a low valley, its bottom too far away to show shadows. Above it all and not knowing how he got there, he swelled with the power of his vantage. This place belongs to Hoolow, alone, he thought, and then he remembered the vision that had brought him to this place, a true vision, and he became more exulted until the puddle in his numbed gut shifted and made itself felt. Shivering with reawakened sensation, his stomach contracted, forcing its remaining contents into his throat. He heaved a black spew off the edge of the cliff, went to his knees and pressed his palms to his sweating forehead. His stomach pulsed, and he choked up mouthfuls of vile-tasting bile after which his innards seemed to return to a state of sedation. The cool air moving over the mouth of the cave refreshed him. He lay down so that, looking at an angle, he could watch the moon descend. Its light bathed his face and soothed him to sleep.

Someone pounded the top of his head with a rock, and he woke up flailing at his attacker. He rolled over the uneven floor of the cave, bruising his sides until he found his footing and stood up blinking in the dim light. He swayed, unsteady on his feet, and received another jolt on the head. He spun to face his assailant and caught a blinding blow. His hands flew to his crown in a defensive gesture. They sunk into the matted cloud of his hair, but discovered no injury. He steadied his head on his neck and felt the persistent throbbing that had only seemed like external blows. He took a tentative step, and the reverberation of impact that surged up his body threatened to dislodge the top of his head. He screeched at the pain, and its echo pierced his skull. He bit his lips and stumbled headlong to the mouth of the cave, where he leaned against the wall and opened his eyes to a view of the valley illuminated below. It made the pain tolerable.

Level with the mouth of the cave was a twisted tree, growing from a crack in a wide expanse of exposed gray bedrock. It seemed like such an unlikely spot for life to flourish that Hoolow was drawn to investigate. As he approached, a long dark stain became visible on the rock above the tree. Recognizing it and realizing his thirst in the same instant, he issued a delighted hoo as if there were others nearby with whom he wished to share his good fortune. He found a toehold in the crack, and bracing his other foot against a tree root, he leaned his body forward, a hand on either side of the dark slick. He pressed his tongue to the cool wet surface of the rock and satisfied his thirst. Next he held the edge of his cupped palm against the rockface and watched it filled by the translucent trickle. He massaged the moisture into his forehead and the back of his neck, reveling in the cool relief it afforded him. When he looked back toward the opening of the cave, he saw that it was deep and black and felt the sting of excitement. He'd spent the night among the disembodied animals. They'd possessed him, and he had survived. He felt brave and contemptuous of his tribemates' superstitions.

Hoolow set about moving the loose rocks from the floor of the cave to make it more livable. His stomach felt light but still queasy, and the enthusiastic exertion extracted its toll. His knees wobbled as he leaned back against the outside wall and examined the landscape once again. He needed food. He made his way over to the tree and drank for a second time that morning. He scoured the area for edible plants and found several but none of the nuts he needed to satisfy his hunger. He returned to his cave carrying bundles of sticks and branches to build a fire. As he approached, the opening looked darker than it had before, and his stomach lurched. He was determined not to give into his fear. After all, he'd already spent one night in the cave. Would the visions assail him as they did the night before? He built up the fire, and while sitting amongst the flickering shadows, heard noises, squeaks and rustles, from deep in the cave. He felt rather than instigated the movement of his body, rocking forward at the hips, swaying back with lifted chin. The sounds he made echoed back a panoply of voices, and he could not be sure all of them were his own. Were there humans among the bodiless animals? They, too, must long for company.

Hunger forced him to fashion a snare by looping a flexible reed into a slipknot. A rabbit could fit its forelegs through, but the movement would cause the loop to tighten. Further struggle could only cause more constriction, and if Hoolow checked his trap before a jackal could find it, he would have fresh meat enough for two meals as well as some soft fur to cushion the places in the cave where he liked to sit.

He set the trap early in the morning so the sun would have ample time to melt away his traces. He tied his snare to a bush that was scattered round with rabbit pellets, a place they must like to shade themselves at midday. He returned early in the afternoon to discover the rabbit squeezed tight around the shoulders, its forelegs suspended as it executed short shallow intakes of breath. Its situation was impossible. If it lived long enough it could only hope to be rent alive by a predator, and yet it burned with desire to live. Its eyes were dim, already blind to Hoolow's approach, but when he grasped it by the ears, its back legs bounded, and he had to struggle to maintain his grip. As quickly as he could, he twisted its neck until he heard the snap that caused its body to go limp. He loosed the snare and left it there uncoiled, tainted by the smell of death that rendered it useless. He thought how much easier this task of procuring meat would be if he could hear the voices of the animals the way his tribemates described them. He would never have suspected they spoke thusly, "life is given," if he had not been told, for by all appearances every animal he'd seen butchered had fought against it.

As he drank of the rabbit's blood, he imagined its life force filling him. Since his vision of the disembodied animals, he knew this life force had a shape—the shape of the animal it once animated. Drinking its blood was akin to swallowing it whole. Hoolow then broke apart its body and set it over the fire.

He wondered how his own death would come. Would he fight? If he could just go quietly, lay his head down in the cave and be taken in his sleep without waking. But it was never that way. No predator was ever so quick. The girl must have suffered, so why shouldn't he? The pain terrified him. And what would come next? He'd never thought of what the moment after death would be like. Every creature fought so hard against it, it could not be good. Did the pain go on and on? This was something the people of his tribe never talked about. The people who were once there were sometimes gone and they never returned, like the girl. She would never return, nor would he, but there was a difference. She lay under the rocks he'd piled above her, while he drank the blood of a rabbit, taking its life so that he could live. Was this a fair thing? The rabbit had not given its permission. Did Hoolow have a right to live? If he'd stayed with the tribe, then this question would never have occurred to him. His life had a function within the tribe—he hunted, he built up the fire— the same as he did for himself. But his was just one life. To the tribe he must be dead. By now they had no expectation of him ever returning. So why persist in living at all? With his belly full, he felt drowsy, and it was good to lie down and stretch his body.

The rabbit sought its vengeance in Hoolow's dream. It chased him through the brush. He bounded on all fours, his perspective shrinking until he was close to the ground, a rabbit himself. He felt himself pulled up. All the air squeezed out of him as the snare tightened around his chest. He struggled breathlessly, and then, out of the haze of panic that surrounded him, he caught a whiff of his tribe. Hoolow, the rabbit, relaxed. Everything would be all right now. He blinked his eyes clear and looked up into the face of the smiling young hunter, who was reaching out a hand to him. As soon as Hoolow felt his fingers close on his neck, he realized their intent and reacted with frantic kicks; his panic was enough to wrestle him out of sleep to discover his legs scissoring against the floor of the cave while his heart hammered.

Night had fallen, and the fire had gone out. There had been no one to tend it while he slept and dreamed. He reassured himself with a careful review of the dreamlike qualities of his recent experience, but he could not shake off his fear in the dark. His fright was exacerbated by the noises from deeper in the cave and canine howls outside it. There was nowhere safe for him. He got to his knees and moved his hands over the cave floor, finding the warm spot where the fire had been. He blew at the cooling embers but failed to ignite the faintest red glow. He fumbled his hands through the dark until he found the two dry sticks he reserved for the purpose of starting fires. He tried to force calmness upon himself as he twisted one stick into the other in the way necessary to make a spark. Out of the corner of his eye he thought he saw a shadow move across the mouth of the cave, but he would not allow himself to be distracted from his task. He smelled smoke and redoubled the speed of his twisting, unconscious of the threatening sweat that dripped from his forehead. He did not let his fear lead him to smother the delicate flame when it appeared. He caged it with tinder while blowing a stream of life-giving oxygen. It crackled, warming his face, and he moved behind it. Ha! He shouted, waving his arms in the air, facing down the empty mouth of the cave. The thought struck him, what if the real threat came from what was behind him? He lifted a burning branch from the flames and whirled it around to illuminate the deeper darkness. The light reached only a feeble distance into the rock tunnel. Everything beyond it remained black.

Through the following days his fear of night lingered in the back of his chest, ready to leap forward and grab hold of his heart at any sudden movement caught in the corner of his eye. All the provocations turned out to be rabbits and ground squirrels and other small creatures he failed to notice while in an ordinary state. Now he was so timorous it was hard to make any progress in foraging past the rock spring.

A reconnaissance of the immediate area revealed no other suitable shelter than the cave, and so the prospect of having to return to it at the end of daylight hung over his every step. Unable to concentrate on anything else, he sat under a tree to contemplate his situation. The sun crept by overhead as he sat in the shade, needing to keep his tired eyes open for predators. He thought again about the possibility of his death. It had to happen sometime. Why not sooner rather than later? He could face this final fear head on and find out what it was all about. He thought of the disembodied animals—would he become one? Would he be forced into the deepest depths of the cave? What if the rabbit still wanted its revenge? And all the other animals he'd helped to kill in his lifetime? But they'd all given their permission. So he'd been told. Death seemed to him more perilous than life.

He was so tired he fell asleep under the tree, and when he awoke in the evening, unmolested, the thought of reversing his waking and sleeping pattern occurred to him. He was sure he would still be able to complete his foraging because his night vision was good. As darkness spread out, it reached over the horizon to pull whatever lurked beyond it into the invisible field surrounding him. Hoolow realized that the only possible protection was three walls of rock and a fire; he plodded toward another night of rocking and chanting.

How had it happened that on the night of his magnificent vision, he'd survived the night so triumphantly? The vision had given him the incredible power of transformation. He had been invincible, and after, despite the sickness, he had continued exercising with vigor; only subsequent nights in the cave had worn him down. It seemed likely that his courage could be revamped by another, similar vision.

He searched for the plant and soon found it growing out from beneath a rock. It spread out its grizzled leaves in invitation, but he gazed upon it with revulsion. Sight of it could not help but recall the initial cramps, and the violent vomiting and astounding headache that followed his vision. He could never push the offending plant past his lips again.

He walked away from it, remembering the sound of his mother's voice, saying "don't eat." He had given no credence to the voice, because its words had appeared inside of him and had no aural quality. How could that be? What sort of thing resided within him that could speak without sound? He reflected on his earliest childhood memories. They were awash with colors, sounds and smells taking form, and he had been consumed by the task of making sense of it all. There had been no time for thoughts. Something inside shifted after the death of his mother. Glimmers of thoughts had existed while she was alive, but after her death they grew to dominate his life.

He'd been aware of his difference from an early age and searched for signs of similar internal activity amongst the others. He would say, "It speaks without a voice."

"What speaks?" had been their natural question for which he had no answer.

It appeared that none of his fellows had undergone a transformation of "thinking," and thus he couldn't help but see himself as an anomaly, a somehow malformed human struggling against an onslaught of thoughts. The rest of his tribe were like the other animals, who acted in the present, where every sight and sound and smell intruded on one another in glaring color. They were absorbed in sorting their perceptions in order to make sense of their environment, whereas for Hoolow, the sorting seemed to be taking place in a remote part of his being. He only received pertinent information scrubbed clean of confounding sensory data. The sensory data itself was categorized by receptor, so if his nose was the first to detect it, he only registered smell and did not bother joining it to its concomitant color and sensation. This new mode of perception was so efficient that it left a space inside of him. The space filled with every manner of speculation.

Hoolow climbed to the top of the ridge. The sun behind him cast long shadows that did not yet reach to where he could see the mouth of his cave, a dark pit sunken into the valley's opposing wall. He forced himself to imagine crawling into it for shelter. He'd been using it night after night, and despite the noises, he'd not come to any harm. He sat and watched the long shadows stretch toward the cave. Soon they would reach the top of the facing ridge, and it would be night. If he sat any longer he'd be alone in the wide-open darkness, filled with hungry predators. The thought pushed him to his feet. The cave could not be worse, and he moved toward it on heavy feet. He reached the valley floor and was about to begin his ascent to the cave, when a black plume poured out of its mouth. He fell back on his heels. The cloud moved over him and spread out in all directions, fragmenting into flapping black bits. Whispers of air flitted passed his cheeks and lifted the hair on top of his head as they wheeled over in jerky flight. Bats, he thought. Bats! He laughed and eased onward feeling jolly.

Safely in the cave, sitting before a fire, he surprised himself with his compulsion for rocking. He concentrated on holding himself still, but his body seemed determined to sway; if for a moment he lost awareness of controlling it, it started up again. He heard the meaningless chant rise from his lungs and echo down the tunnel to mingle with the squeaks and scratching he now knew to be the sounds of bats, but this knowledge did not erase their sinister character. Weary of controlling his tic, he gave into what had become the natural motion of his body. He lost himself in the repetitive cadence of his voice and later roused to the thought that his life had no purpose. Death seemed to be the natural territory of his thoughts.

His inability to fashion another snare out of fear of retribution from its victim conspired with his failure to find any of the satisfying nuts to which he was accustomed, causing his gut to groan incessantly. His bowels were loose from the quantities of greens he'd consumed, and he found himself having to squat without cover, which embarrassed him despite there being no one around to see. The only solution was scavenging for meat as he'd done with his fellow hunters. It would require that he be wary of returning predators as he was without the help of his tribemates or any hint of the hues that had linked them to sounds and smells, because since his magnificent vision, his remaining colors had dried up. He experienced no more unexpected flashes and had to rely on a clearly delineated sight, where there were no blendings of sound and smell.

He searched the sky for circling buzzards, waiting to see one dive before approaching. He didn't want to surprise a feasting lion, and with no weapon, he had no choice but vigilance. The tall grass obscured the ground in front of him. He picked up a rock as he drew closer, but then heard the great birds squawking amongst themselves and relaxed. They argued but would not fight. He threw the rock into their tangle and seeing them break apart, rushed in amongst them, shouting, "Ha, ha," and throwing up his hands. Never before having performed this act alone, he was surprised at how quickly the birds scattered.

It was a large carcass, and the exposed bones were easy to strip, with a few tender morsels still clinging here and there. Thinking of the power of the beast that must have brought it down caused a deep apprehension. He ate without tasting, his attention focused on scanning the surrounding grass for movement and analyzing every sound for a possible threat. He stopped before he was full, the snap of a large twig jolting him into a sprint. He'd gone a good distance before chancing a backward glance to confirm he was not being pursued. He rested his palms on his bent knees and hung his head forward with relief. The meat in his belly threatened to heave itself out of its container. He concentrated on holding it down and once it was settled, walked back to his cave, feeling some strength in his accomplishment.

Once back in the security of the cave, a new craving seized him. He built up the fire until it roared, flickering shadows all about the cave walls. Its smoke bent along the ceiling and poured out of the mouth of the cave. It was hot, and his eyes watered. He picked up a torch and headed for the passageway at the back. The space was narrow. If he extended his arms to either side he could press his palms flat against both walls. He held his torch high to increase the circle of light that proceeded him into the darkness, but as he moved deeper the ceiling descended. He lowered his torch until he was holding it before his face. Its smoke pulled back toward the opening of the cave, pouring over his face, hot and stinging, blinding him to every feature of the passage. He felt challenged. Rocks piled on the floor required him to scramble, working to squeeze himself through cramped spaces. The torch became unwieldy. He decided he could best maneuver himself over a new obstacle if he laid his torch down, and once through, pulled it after him. He first pushed the torch through the narrow opening. Beyond the rock, the passage opened slightly before tapering into a darkness his light couldn't penetrate. It was impossible for him to tell how much further the tunnel dove into the earth. He looked back over the way he'd come. He must have made some unnoticed turns, because the fire he'd built up in the outside room was not visible. He propped his torch against the rock. He did not anticipate the floor on the other side being half a leg's length lower. He dropped headfirst, catching himself with his hands and executing a somersault to come to rest in a seated position. In front of him was pure blackness. Looking over his shoulder, he could see the light of his torch blinking over the opening he'd just passed through. He stood and reached over the rock, but standing lower than he'd expected, the torch was outside of his grasp. He thought of climbing back and finding another way to proceed or else turning back. He had investigated a good bit. He would be better able to tackle further exploration the next night. He realized with surprise how calm he was. He'd never been so deep in the cave before. The bats having exited for the night, it was quiet, the air still. His eyes began to adjust to the feeble light of the torch, and he could see down the passage he'd come; its corrugated walls and uneven floor wavered in his vision, winking in and out of illumination. Then the torch went out. The darkness was total. He stood still. A bead of sweat curled over his temple, cooling in its descent. Beneath his fingertips the rock was solid, coated with a fine layer of dust. He lowered himself to the floor and leaned his back against the rock so he wouldn't lose it in the darkness and forget which rock he needed to climb over to get out. He was not ready to get out, although his heart seemed to be urging him in that direction with its furious beats. Without his sight to distract him, his breaths sounded loud, external. He squeezed his eyes shut and opened them again, registering no difference. An eerie calmness pervaded him. Flashes of color sprang out of the darkness, agglutinated and then teased themselves apart, the individual threads swirling away and growing fainter at the edges until they melted back into invisibility. He laughed with delight, and the unexpected sound frightened him. He pressed against the rock as his voice reverberated back from the tunnel. It seemed to be illuminated, a cloud of coruscating colors rumbling up from the further depths of the cave. It reached him, enveloped him, and he tumbled into its vortex, at first groping for the rock against which he reclined but then pushing off from it, increasing the spin of his flight. The colors fluxed about him, and he laughed as he rolled over in the air. He felt a great suction at his feet and knew he was being pulled deeper into the passage, but he did not resist. He extended his arms to the sides and felt the walls of the cave sliding by beneath his fingertips. The cloud, which was his vehicle, rotated to bring him to vertical and then unfolded. Far from dissipating, it reconfigured into a landscape of solid images that were like nothing he'd ever seen. Everything—trees, birds, and previously unknown heavenly bodies—vibrated with color. He took a step and looked back to see his footprint sink in the glowing red earth. He lifted his hand in front of his face as if to test the darkness and was entranced by the tiny beads of color that traversed the lines in his palm. A colony of beings was constructing another world beneath his digits. His head whirled at the magnitude of this idea, and he fell headfirst into it, feeling his palm slap against his forehead as he plunged, and it was with regret that he fell further because he'd wanted to explore the first beautiful landscape. The second one was less vivid. Images were delineated by a hazy outline of dots that trailed from one object to the next in a continuous thread his eyes seemed compelled to follow. There were animals here, large grazing animals he'd hunted in his former life with the tribe. They engaged in ordinary activities, browsing and flicking their tails at imaginary flies, but they did it all above where he thought the ground should be. It felt as if his feet were standing lower. He bent his knees and took a short hop to test it. It was solid. He looked at the animals moving about with no constraints of space, and the sight, which had fascinated, suddenly made him dizzy. He needed to feel the ground. He knelt and placed his hands against the cool floor of the cave. Yes, it was real. Solid, he thought. He ran his hands out in all directions, feeling for debris before stretching himself out supine. Now he felt secure, more at ease. The animals that had been moving all around him plodded up an invisible hill that rose above him. They stood along its curve, a parabola of grazing animals arcing over his belly, contained within his line of sight. It pleased him to watch their gentle movements. A buck lifted its head to look at him. What had been an outline snapped into sharp focus, and he could see into the animal's moist eyes. He felt his eyelids drooping and forced them open. The vision was too beautiful to sleep, but eventually weariness overtook him.

He awoke in total darkness and was panicked. He didn't allow his fear to cause any movement in his body. He needed to be methodical. There was no telling how deep into the passage his vision had carried him, but if he could find the rock he'd climbed over to get to this space, he would be safe. He felt certain his hands would recognize it if he could remain calm and allow them to feel their way. He got to his knees and crawled, sweeping his hands in front of him. How far? he wondered. He found the wall of the cave and moved his hands up it to confirm that it was not a simple obstruction, but should he move to the right or left? He had no idea how many times his vision had turned him. He moved to his left. After a few paces the side of his foot hit the rock. It seemed impossible that he'd hardly moved since the start of his vision, but he felt certain that it was *the* rock. He passed his hands over its surface, recognizing it. He hoisted himself up to the narrow opening between it and the ceiling and reaching down, encountered his spent torch. All the tension in his body oozed out, and he slid through, kicking his feet at the last so that he landed in a pile on the floor. He laughed and rolled back up the passageway he'd traveled the night before. He found his feet, and trailing his hand against the wall for guidance, he ran through the blackness, elated. He made a turn, and gray light appeared ahead. He squinted his eyes against it but didn't slow his progress; he made another turn, and the full light of mid-morning streamed into his eyes. He raced to the opening, his eyes squeezed tight against the glare, but he'd become accustomed to moving blindly. He burst from the mouth of the cave and paused to lean against its outside wall. He tilted his head back to feel the warmth of the sun on his face. His eyelids glowed red, and slowly he opened them. The light at first was painful. His eyes watered, but he persisted by degrees until he was looking out over the valley below him. He threw up his hands and laughed with joy.

He waited for nightfall to make another excursion into the deep cave. As the time grew near, he felt nauseated and quivery with anticipation. Once on the other side of the big rock, he waited for the cloud of colors, staring hard down the dark tunnel, and then he remembered that he needed to laugh. His laughter had brought it the night before. The thought itself was funny, and he cackled. The cloud whooshed toward him. Its bright interior unspooled, revealing bejeweled trees and a sky hung with nebulous ornaments, twirling in time to his heartbeats. His eyes were dazzled. His hand twitched. It itched. He felt there was something in his palm that he needed to look at. It crawled, inching up his forearm until he could stand it no longer. He looked into his hand and fell between the lines, back into the darkness of the cave, where only the outlines of animals were illuminated. He watched them grazing placidly until he became agitated. He closed his eyes and willed himself to sleep.

Hoolow emerged from the cave while the moon was still high and full, but the next night it was a thin blade hanging low in the sky. The familiar cycle of the moon's parturition had become disjointed. Although troubled, the cave beckoned, and Hoolow could not resist its call. Moons had already passed beyond his counting, and so he determined not to notice their confused cycle. In contrast to his turbulent nights, his days developed a pattern: he emerged from the cave elated by his night's vision, but as the morning progressed, depression crept up in him. It started somewhere around his knees, causing him to slog through his morning rounds in search of food, making this potentially pleasant activity a chore; by midday the depression reached the top of his head, settling him into a funk. He slunk beneath a tree and waited for the sun to fall; all the colors surrounding him seemed dull and lifeless. If his eye chanced upon a pebble of particular brightness, he dug a slight depression in the dirt and set the pebble at its center, hoping its contrast with the dull ground would make it sparkle. It never satisfied.

He wondered if he could discuss his visions with others what they would say. He observed his new visions unlike the plant induced one in which he had assumed an ever changing role. In all the other visions he'd heard described, the teller became every actor in his story. He realized he had stumbled upon a unique experience, something else that distinguished him from his tribemates.

The bright flowers blooming on a cactus caught his attention. If he squinted at them and cupped his hands around his face to obscure his peripheral vision, they almost popped like the colors of his visions, but he could not achieve the exact effect and so his pleasure was brief. His thoughts turned inevitably toward his nighttime forays into the deeper cave. He craved his visions. An attempt during the daylight aggravated the resident population of bats, whose erratic bombardments were enough distraction to prevent the visions from materializing. He must wait for their exodus at dusk. He grew impatient as the sun dipped lower in the sky, and he often attempted to sleep then in order to be fresh for his nocturnal excursions.

Fresh as he was, he did not have the will to resist the itch in the palm of his hand. Invariably he looked, cursing himself in the act as he was sucked out of the beautiful garden in which he longed to linger. Every glimpse of it seemed briefer, and the long stretches he spent with the hollow outlines of the animals grew boring. As if grown used to his presence, they ignored him. He drew his hands through them, breaking them apart, but they coalesced back into their original forms and continued to graze the invisible ground cover as if never interrupted. He lay down, trying to absorb himself in their subtle movements—they were fascinating in their nature— but he had seen them too many times. He groped for the rock, but his hands had grown fat in the dark; they were insensitive cushions, preventing him from feeling the specific contours that identified the rock for which he searched. He struggled to calm himself with the knowledge that the situation would resolve itself. He hadn't lost his way in the cave yet; he always awoke in the same spot as if he never traveled during of one his visions. In the morning, he thought, after sleep.

As the moon continued its erratic waning and waxing, another disturbing aftereffect joined with the depression to make his days truly miserable: a relentless headache. It throbbed through his rounds. He lay his skull back against the trunk of a tree and felt the bumps of bark like boulders. No patch of ground was smooth enough to cradle him. He shivered in his ache and considered giving up the visions altogether, but the possibility of remaining in the beautiful garden for a longer period still enticed him. With the full motivation of pain to spur him, he set his determination on a final trip.

Inside the unfolded cloud, he shook his wrist. The itch crept up his forearm, but he felt powerful in his ability to resist looking at it. He frolicked amongst the trees, trailing his fingertips around their textured bark that was like layers of multi-colored chips of flint. He looked up into their branches and saw the shapes formed by their interstices shifting and changing color. His laughter ruffled the leaves. They turned, glinting from green to blue. He walked to the edge of the garden, beyond which was blackness. He stuck his hand into it and watched it disappear in darkness up to his elbow. There was no escape from this vision—but who would want to escape it? A purple and white cluster of globose fruit caught his eye. It was just within reach, and he fondled it, marveling at each little orb nestled next to another. He picked one, and expecting a burst of ambrosial flavor, he slid it onto his tongue with relish. His lips closed around it, but its flavorless skin refused to break under the pressure of his palate. Instead the sensation of roundness seemed to expand outside of his mouth, enclosing him; he feared suffocation and spat. The purple ball bounced away from him, trailing a series of perfect arches. He looked to the heavenly bodies that had previously pulsed to the pounding of his heart and saw that they were stagnant. He didn't want to look anymore, and yet the colors glowed, demanding his attention. He stared until his eyes burned. He tried closing them, but the colors buzzed through the capillaries on the insides of his eyelids. He looked into his palm. It was paler than the rest of his flesh but the lines were merely indentations without color. He sat, worse than bored, with the beginnings of fear. He longed for sleep to release him from this vision. He rested his elbows on his knees and his chin in his cupped hands and sighed. His exhalation was a blue vapor. He watched it dissipate without interest. He breathed out again. The blue cloud expanded outward from the tip of his nose. This is it, he thought. This is all there is. His desire for further visions dissolved as he watched the blue vapor of his breath. He realized he'd have to find another way of life.

Alone in his cave the next night, he remembered the sight of his breath. He sat and exhaled. He felt the breath leaving his body, and although he couldn't see it, he imagined it as a blue puff. He drew in a new breath and felt his body expand. He became absorbed in the sensation. He was calmed. No thoughts encroached on his measured breaths. His rocking ceased, and he became still.

This new calmness did not extend into his daylight hours, when he longed for some bit of excitement. While walking, he spotted a carcass draped over the branch of a tree. A leopard, who hunted by night, had left it there for safe keeping during the day. Hoolow felt the hair on his arms prickling. The big cat was undoubtedly close by, guarding its kill in sleep. The carcass was fresh, and the tender pink meat smelled pungent in the sun. He felt himself drawn to it. It was the risk that excited him as much as the meat. He fitted his feet to the crooks of branches and ascended. Wrapping one arm around the trunk, he leaned his body out, letting one foot dangle while he extended his other arm toward the carcass. A yellow flash appeared at the corner of his vision. It felt as if the tree shook, and his free foot pawed the air for purchase. His arm pinwheeled, throwing him off balance so that he fell, his fingernails clawing at the trunk as he broke through branches; one jagged end tore into his right calf before he hit the ground, landing on his side and rolling into a tight ball, expecting the heavy cat to land on top of him. He waited. He tentatively released his arms and looked about. The carcass was still above, but there was no cat anywhere. The yellow flash must have been his imagination; the realization caused a swell of nervous laughter. It died away as he stood and examined his body, for the first time noticing the damage done to his leg. The gash ran the length of his calf muscle; it was open and bleeding. The wound seemed to eat up his attention; the environment receded, everything outside of himself becoming distant. A drumming in his ears muffled the sounds he was usually keen to. He took a step and felt dizzy. He paused to collect his sense, and the full impact of his situation hit him: he was injured and exposed. The cat could not be far away; it may even be stalking him now. He needed to get to his cave; he needed to get there quickly and with confidence. He walked, careful to show no favor to his wounded leg. So long as he focused on his objective, the limb remained numb. Upon reaching the cave, he built up a roaring fire and lay down next to it. He began to sweat, and his leg awoke with startling pain. He gritted his teeth and gripped his sides as he struggled against the memory of his mother's gangrenous stink.

He searched his thoughts for distraction and settled on a replaying of the day's earlier events. He approached the tree with its dangling carcass and was reinvigorated by its odor of fresh meat. He drew himself up its branches, moving hand over hand until the carcass was within reach. He found a foothold in the air and used both hands to roll the carcass off the branch. It thumped pleasantly on the ground, and he drifted down after it, not bothering to look around for the cat before feasting. The skin was thin enough to tear with his fingertips. The meat was almost as tender. Its fibers dissolved in his mouth without chewing. He'd never tasted anything so delicious. He twisted a limb at the knee joint, and it broke from the rest of the body without resistance. He gnawed at its broken end, the flesh pulling away as he nibbled to the foot, expecting to stop at the ankle, beyond which would be the unpalatable hoof, but his lips continued on, biting for the pleasure of it, as he was already sated. His eyelids drooped. He licked his lips a final time and looked at the cleaned white bone. His eyes slid down to where his hand gripped the arch of a delicate brown foot. Its toes stretched and wriggled; the girl's laughter rang from the branches above him.

The fire sputtered, and he had to force himself out for more wood, wary while exposed. He built up the fire, and as soon as it roared, felt the throbbing in his leg. He examined his wound, despaired and fell into another fitful sleep.

He felt her hand on his forehead and opened his eyes to see a face he'd mulled in his memory a thousand times. She'd receded so far into his past it was hard to believe she was here now, and yet he was not startled. Her eyes crinkled at the corners, and the wrinkles bracketing her lips pushed back to her ears as she smiled at Hoolow, her last child. She knew he was different from all her others, and yet she seemed to be the only one who noticed. He was rarely startled by flashes of color but responded to the suggestions of his fellows. She could see the colors blossoming in his head, but he did not move his eyes around, following them the way the others did, herself included. He watched inwardly, in some way utilizing an interior mechanism, the workings of which she tried to imagine, for she'd had her own glimmers of an internal self. There were times when she watched the others watching her as she told her dream, and their reactions were more interesting than what she was telling. She listened to her own voice spooling it out, and it seemed distant, other; she had wondered, where is that sound coming from? She could almost see herself reflected in the staring eyes of the crowd before her. The way they looked at her, absorbed in her—no, she told herself, absorbed in the telling—but what was this other thing trying to step out of the shadows of her story? It was an otherness of which she was aware and could address and respond to without literal sound issuing from her lips. She had been distracted from contemplating it further by her leaping cherub, Hoolow, but the mysterious thing about him made her confident that he would be able to unravel her inner mystery—or at least his own.

Hoolow realized that he was hearing her thoughts as if she were inside of him, standing alongside of his self, his interior self, the other inside him who thought and was separate from his body, who did as he told it to do, but sometimes moved of its own volition, as it had done under the influence of the weed that had transformed him, allowing him to fly and swim and see colors more vivid than ever in his childhood. He thought how the perceptions of his body were different from the perceptions of this inner self that had the ability to experience great visions, while his body traveled long distances or remained lying on the cave floor. He watched as his mother stood and stepped back from where he was lying, looking up at her belly, swollen with child as he remembered it; she moved gracefully, unhindered by her girth. He blinked and saw himself as two separate beings joined together, one inside the other. His interior self was the progenitor of the thoughts that plagued him and set him apart from his fellows. He knew his former tribemates were incapable of seeing the distinction between their two selves, or maybe they were singular, like the animals, who remained whole until death and never experienced, as he did, a clumsy connection between disparate parts of self. His mother smiled proudly, and he awoke tingling with the aftershock of fresh insight. He examined his wound again and took note of the thick scab that stretched from skin to skin. There was no pus. He sniffed, and the only smell was of himself.

*   *   *

He bent the snare to the desired shape and suspended it the right distance from the ground to catch a rabbit, imagining its succulent meat without a tremor, the idea of retribution resolved. The wrathful rabbit of his dream was no more a reality than the leopard that had chased him and caused the injury now healing at a fantastic rate thanks to the ministrations of his mother.

He was determined to watch his snare so that its victim would not suffer longer than necessary. He settled himself some distance behind it. The moment his snare tripped, the shrub to which he'd attached it would shake, and he could retrieve his quarry. He lifted the edge of his scab; an ooze of blood appeared, and he mashed the crust back into place. He licked his finger, and the flavor caused him to salivate, the fresh meal of rabbit leaping to the forefront of his imagination. He watched the shrub, but soon laid his head back and laced his fingers across his grumbling belly. With his eyes closed, the sun reminded him of his mother's hand pressed to his cheek. He felt a connection to her, almost as if he'd just left the nest of the tribe instead of his solitary cave, where the fire had probably already snuffed. But his mother had not actually appeared to him, as he knew she was dead. She was no more real than the rabbit or the leopard or the visions of other animals that appeared deep in the cave, yet he associated his vision of her with the rapid healing of his leg, and therefore she seemed to be of a substance none of his earlier visions had demonstrated. He decided to call the substance, "spirit," and wondered if perhaps his own inner self would outlive his body and become spirit after his death. Was there some place where spirits resided akin to the realm of disembodied animals in the deep cave?

A violent rattle from the shrub shocked him from his rumination. He leapt to his feet and ran to the side of the bush, where he was greeted by a surprising hiss. Leaning forward and keeping the rest of his body well back, he peeked around to his snare. Amidst the writhing fur, it was hard to make out what he had caught. It was something smaller than a rabbit and far more energetic. Its striped body did backflips, stirring the dust as it mewled in indignation. Hoolow watched for several minutes before the twisting mass paused long enough for a glimpse that revealed a small cat, a baby, snagged by a curious front paw. It was a bit of bad luck. Not only was his snare ruined, but the cat's predator stink would be everywhere. He'd have to find a new hunting spot. He contemplated eating the kitten, as he suspected killing it would require no more effort than figuring out how to release it without having his forearms torn to ribbons, but predator meat was foul. He hoped it would tire, but its vocalizations soon turned distressing. He scanned the vicinity for signs of its mother, who would be a small animal herself, one of which he was not afraid, but if she was about, she did not show herself. Out of compassion, he knelt into the fray. The cat reared back from his hands, horripilating its fur, but it did not attack. Hoolow loosened the snare; the cat drew out its paw and sat back on its haunches, blinking at him.

Hoolow stood and turned, but after a few paces, looked back to see the cat still sitting beneath the branches of the shrub. Hoolow parted his lips and hissed through clenched teeth. He waved the back of his hand at it. The kitten took a bumbling step backward and fell to its side, quickly righting itself as if embarrassed by its inept locomotion. Hoolow laughed and looked for a moment longer before turning for the second time. The cat chased him, leaping at his ankles. He tried again to shoo it, but the animal persisted, catching hold of his heel with its claws and causing him to yelp and shake his foot. After the cat dropped, he hadn't the heart to kick it away, and so it pursued him to his cave.

After nightfall the tiny cat stalked the shadows on the far side of the flame, and he couldn't help but watch its tense, focused movements. It reminded him of the hunters moving in a single, alert body tuned to every nuance of the environment. The kitten pounced on an invisible prey and examined its empty paws. Hoolow laughed. It was strange to hear his laughter reverberate in the chamber, emphasizing its hollowness. The cat, too, grew still and raised its hackles. Hoolow sympathized, but he was beyond fearing the emptiness of the cave. He let his eyelids fall and began the rocking that soothed. The chant came up from his lungs and swirled about the chamber, muffling any sounds that might creep in. He forgot everything, but existed within the sound and mechanical sway of his body. He felt a paw on his thigh and then the small, sinuous body sliding into this lap. The chanting stopped, and he felt a ticking purr against his lower belly. He ceased his rocking so that he could focus on the new sensation. He breathed, feeling the way his belly abutted the obstruction. The blue breath flowed out of him, and he drew it back, deep, down into his lower body, where it moved out into the cat with its steady, soothing vibration.

With the discontinuation of his vision-seeking in the deep cave, the moon resumed it familiar cycle, and he no longer needed to imagine the blue color of his breath. The vapor entered him as a clear nothingness that swept away his anxieties on its inexorable retreat. Behind his eyelids was a cool, arid darkness, unmuddled by the thoughts that had been his curse. He relished it, and in the moments when he walked, gathering the plants he liked or setting snares for rabbits, who died swiftly in his hands, he watched the cat frisk alongside his ankles and bound into the brush after prey too small to be of interest to him, and he thought about how his nature had been transformed. Before his isolation, his thoughts had controlled him, coursing through his mind, causing whirlpools of emotion that had spun him into chaos. Now he had constructed a channel through which his thoughts flowed without detours. Although he couldn't stop the flow, it had slowed to where there was hardly a ripple, and the days slid by one into the next with a minimum of thoughts. He looked forward to the moments of sitting, feeling his breath moving in and out, cleansing him. His body felt remote to him in these moments; he was his breath alone.

When the cat had grown big, it only returned to the cave at night; when Hoolow awoke in the morning, it would be curled against his side. He could feel the rhythm of its breaths, quicker than his own even in sleep, palpating its body from within. He eased himself away to avoid waking it, and it squirmed partway onto its back, one leg bent across the upper part of its face as if shielding its eyes from sunlight. Hoolow paused a moment to peer down at it, admiring. The tender emotion he felt confused him. It was an adult cat, too small to cause him any harm, but he thought its resemblance to the larger animal that had killed the girl and menaced the tribe's dreams should cause him to find it distasteful, yet he could not help but feel for it as he imagined he would feel for the youngest members of the tribe—if he were still with them.

He emerged from his cave and stretched in the sunlight before bending to examine the scar on his leg; he wondered if it had actually been his spirit mother who healed him. Perhaps the scar would have healed as fast without the vision. It might not have been as bad as he originally thought. It was the heightened state of fear that made him see it as a nasty gash, when maybe all it was, was a simple cut, yet the scar it left behind was impressive.

He filled his belly while the sun was still low enough for him to enjoy its slanting rays. He sat on a rock next to a lizard, one perhaps too cold to flit away. It raised itself on its front legs and expanded the blue flap of skin beneath its chin. Hoolow watched, unmoving. The tiny animal lowered itself and cocked an eye over Hoolow's massive bulk, then it seemed content to relax and absorb more of the sun's rays. The essence of the animal seemed to extend beyond the confines of its slender body. On a day when he was famished he would have considered the lizard in terms of palatability, but today he was not hungry, and the lizard seemed to sense that it was safe to remain close by. Hoolow felt that he had a companion in sunbathing and was pleased not to be thought of as threatening. He closed his eyes, but he was alert to the sounds in his environment. The humming of insects grew louder, and embedded in this steady background noise were the calls of birds. As each one sounded, he pictured its particular plumage—a screeching eagle spread its banded tail—and these spontaneous images gave him pleasure. The images faded, and the calls became enmeshed in the steady insect hum. The faint rustle of leaves in a breeze captivated him. The unpredictability of the weak gusts pricked his ears and then rewarded him with the sound of branches brushing against one another. He soon grew accustomed to this pleasure as well, and it was the sensations on his skin that next drew his attention. All the sounds in the environment seemed to collect there, and as he observed their play over the surface of his body, he forgot that they were sounds.

After awhile his skin felt saturated with sensation, and it ceased to be the focus of his attention. He retreated further into himself, passing through a darkened passageway like the one that led to the deeper part of the cave, but he traversed it without a torch and without fear, until he reached a throbbing orb of brilliant light. It sent out white shafts in every direction, and he felt himself incinerated and yet secure in his position on the rock. He opened his eyes to confirm his situation. The sun had moved to warm the back of his head, and when he looked down to where the lizard had been, he saw only his shadow. His legs cramped when he stood, but he was pleased by the sensation. The tingling he felt as he walked was something exciting; although familiar, it was as if he'd never experienced it before. He welcomed the darkness of his cave and was pleased when the cat returned at nightfall, carrying the body of a mouse in its jaws. The cat settled on the far side of the fire and crunched the bones of its prey. When it was done licking its chops, Hoolow watched as it cleaned its face with its forepaws, folding its whiskers across its tongue. When this ablution was complete, the cat moved to Hoolow's side and settled itself with a sigh. Hoolow stroked its fur and lowered his eyelids to the steady vibration of its purr.

Hoolow walked further the next day than he did on most days; he was enjoying the pleasure of his feet slapping against the warm earth, when he heard a sound he hadn't heard since leaving the tribe—a short expiration followed by a long vowel. It was a call he recognized, and he immediately dropped to his haunches. He heard what he knew to be human footsteps, several pairs, and he hunkered behind a rock, chancing a peek when the footsteps stopped and the hoos were soft and reflective. There stood a group of hunters. Hoolow was not afraid, but he kept himself hidden, while he was riveted by their presence. He recognized each of them, although they'd changed considerably. He was most disappointed that the graybeard was not among them.

The young hunter could not be called young anymore. His body was richly burnished by the sun. His expression was one of intensity, and yet he looked untroubled, even serene. He was performing a preassigned duty in the same manner as he'd always performed it. He allowed his senses to guide him. There was scarcely a decision to be made, and the others followed him with confidence, their own senses confirming the correctness of his every move. Once Hoolow had moved in this manner, but he'd struggled to put his thoughts aside to do so. He searched their faces and detected no signs of struggle. He felt more alone than ever.

He stayed hidden behind the rock, even after the hunters had gone. How had he missed the sensation of so many moons passing? He looked down at his body, trying to detect signs of growth. Had his chest grown broader? There was more hair there, which first delighted and then saddened him. If he'd remained with the tribe, such changes would not have gone unnoticed. He missed their teasing. Perhaps now the women would find him more attractive and would signal to him across the fire. He thought of the girl and the simple warmth of her body. His ears ached for their songs. He hummed on the way back to his cave and upon reaching it, burst into song. At first he felt uplifted but then depressed. The tribe moved through the environment with no inner selves to cause feelings of separation between them. This was what he longed for and could perhaps achieve through the dissolution of his own inner self. It seemed to disappear when his thoughts were under his control, but it was a state difficult to maintain. The longing for communion with his fellows struck up a pain in his chest. Was he worthy of their companionship?

When the cat returned that night it looked small and insufficient to calm his ache for fellowship, and so he disdained it. When it moved to crawl into his lap, he shoved it away and didn't watch as it slunk out of the cave. Good riddance, he thought, dirty animal, and he felt regretful. Its warmth could have provided him comfort; he remonstrated himself for pushing it away and was saddened by the knowledge that he'd not yet conquered his impulses. One glimpse of the tribe, and he was his old self again.

When the cat did not come back the next night, he searched for it in despair. He missed his companion desperately and blamed himself for the severance of their relationship, although it was more likely that the animal, having reached the age of maturity, had gone in search of a mate of its own kind. Hoolow had loved the cat and was tortured by the thought that it had gone away thinking otherwise—but this was silly, because the cat did not have thoughts, having no inner self. He was the only being cursed with this particular affliction.

Hoolow could no longer bear his solitude without visions and without the cat to breathe against his side at night. The sounds of the bats disturbed his sleep, and he sat up, rocking, and hated himself for this regression. He recalled how he had flicked his toes to entice the cat to pounce on them and how he had laughed at the feel of its sharp teeth playing over his skin but never puncturing it. How he loved the cat! He missed it and searched for it, but its ways were mysterious to him, more mysterious than his fellow humans had ever been. Having known the animal, he realized that it did have a sort of inner self, but one that was not distinct. It harmonized with its surroundings. Every living thing then began to appear as if it had "self," but one self, shared; their spirits did not become distinct entities until after death. Living, they composed a single body, animated by the life force that was a continuum of spirit. Only he was divorced from it by the mutation of "thinking."

Where once he was filled with peace and acceptance of himself and the world, now, once again, he felt like he was doing battle with it. He could no longer stand to be alone but

longed for the tactile pleasure of the cat's fur. He longed for
the feeling of another's skin rubbed across his skin. He
wanted envelopment within warm, moist skin, to disappear
into it, forget himself. It became his fixation, the only possible
remedy for his new dis-ease: to be obliterated by another's
touch. No vision enticed him; no thoughts of immaterial
comfort soothed him. His skin felt scourged, raw, in need of
another's covering.

His thoughts wearied him, and the pain of his lost cat
was a provocative kind of ache. He felt spurred to pursue
some new course, and it seemed that even while in the midst
of searching for the cat, his thoughts wandered over his
recollections of the faces of the tribe. If he had changed so
much, how much had they? He worried that the tribe would
not recognize him. Would he appear as a stranger in their
midst? Would they accept him? What he wouldn't do to be
accepted back into their fold! He would grovel for their
amusement and absorb their mockery if they would only
welcome him back.

One day he realized he'd wandered farther than the cat
would dare to go, and he kept walking. It was not the cat he
was after anymore. He wasn't convinced of what he sought
until he found the spring, the one where he swam as a child,
and he raced around its perimeter, hooing. When the others
didn't come to his call, he climbed one of the tall boulders he
recognized so well, and from this vantage he took in careful
views of the land. He may have changed, but this place was
the same without a doubt. There was the pile of rock that hid
their shelter. He jumped from the boulder and made his way
toward it. The path that was once pounded smooth by their
feet was cluttered with fallen debris, but he barely noticed;
kicking it aside or climbing over in his haste, he made his way
to the shelter. The area of their fire was still black, but his feet

sunk into the accumulated dust. Some very old-looking nuts had their own coating and lay scattered across the cave floor. He could see the depressions where their bodies had lain. They were shallower, slowly filling up to the level of the floor. He knelt and placed his hand against the black dirt of the old firepit. It was as cold as the air. He wiped his blackened palm across his forehead, where his sweat fixed the charcoal in place, and so marked he made his way down by another worn but recently unused path.

He paused under a rock overhang and looking up, envisioned a younger incarnation of himself gazing down in horror. He stood in a patch of thick grass and plied it with his toes. She would have had children by now, he thought, and his heart clenched anew as he imagined the small, bright-skinned humans who would have squinted up at him with her wide-set eyes. He walked as he had walked carrying her body, heavily, intent on his own exhaustion. His knees ached before he reached the scattered cairn. He looked upon the stones rolled in every direction and felt tears come to his eyes. There was no trace of her in the depression he'd scratched in the earth, not that he'd wanted to look upon her remains, but he'd hoped for a feeling, a sense of her still lingering in this spot; she was no more here than she was anywhere. The grass had grown tall around the site, and he moved through it, bent over, parting the blades and peering down at the ground, looking for he knew not what until a chalk-white stick caught his eye. It was hollow and splintered at both ends, and when he picked it up, a gleaming black beetle poked out its front legs and then pulled them back. Hoolow shook out the bug and crushed it beneath his heel. He wiped its blood on the grass, shuffling his foot back and forth, and held the delicate fragment of bone to his chest. It did not vibrate as he hoped. It remained lifeless in his palm, and as he stared at it, willing some pulse of life to sound from it, a feeling of revulsion overcame him. He let the bone drop and stumbled back from it, his heel catching a rock and tumbling him into the shallow depression he'd dug for the girl. Realizing he lay on the exact spot where he'd applied the pressure that had forced her rigid body into a desired shape, he scrambled away. He sprinted toward the spring and flung himself down at its bank. His face appeared twisted and black. He reared away. He fell on his side and wrapped his arms across his broadened chest. He wept great howling sobs. He wept for the girl, but mostly he wept for himself who'd been alone for so long and was still alone despite the familiarity of his surroundings. They'd never before felt so empty, nor he. When finally he was calm, he hung his head over the spring again; his expression was vague, but the black soot was evident. He was grateful to have some reason to dip his cupped hands into the reflection of his face. He joined his two faces together in cool refreshment, drawing the water to his cheeks over and over, until his skin was stripped bare and felt tight against the breeze.

The sun sank as he walked along the path he'd walked so often to reach the shelter before nightfall, collecting sticks for the fire along the way. He built it up in the place where he'd had so much help building it in the past. He imagined all of their hands reaching out to add fodder to the flame. He heard their laughter between the crackles. He wondered what had prompted their relocation. He thought of the graybeard, missing from the hunting party he'd seen earlier; perhaps the graybeard had fallen ill and died in this shelter. Then the tribe would have feared disease and moved. Animals would have dragged the graybeard's bones from this place. Hoolow crawled across the floor, running his hands over the body-shaped depressions, trying to remember the one the graybeard favored, but his memory was unclear on this point. There was one whose occupants he remembered well—the girl and her mother had slept here with the little sister tucked into a dreaming ball. Hoolow rolled himself into it. All the emotions of the day filled in the space around him, and he did not feel alone. There was a glimmer of hope in him that the others could still be found. He had seen the hunters, and they would not have traveled more than two days' walk for food. He would find the rest of the tribe.

He awoke in a state of confidence and refreshment. The nuts he'd so long craved were easy to find along the edges of a well worn trail. He knew he'd have to leave these traces of humanity if he were to find the tribe's present abode, so as soon as his hunger was sated, he turned into the tall grass. The brush against his legs was a pleasant sensation, especially where it wisped over the smooth skin of his scar. It was an easy walk for which he was well prepared, and although it dragged on past midday with no sign of his tribe, he was not wearied but was drawn to the new spring by the smell of fresh water.

It was deep and banked on one side by basalt blocks. His mouth wetted with anticipation as he approached, but the sparkle of sunlight skipping over the surface of the water caused black spots in his vision. He scrubbed his eyes with the sides of his fists and blinked. A dribble of perspiration wormed over the backward-facing crease of his ear, and he shivered as it dripped from lobe to shoulder. The image of the girl seemed to materialize out of the shimmers of humidity lifting off of the spring. She squatted at its edge, leaning forward on her toes and forearms as she stretched her lips to the surface of the water, her posture like one in the chorus of grasshoppers chirruping in the still air. A gnat flitting in circles about his head seemed to buzz through him as he was paralyzed with shock, too afraid to advance or retreat, afraid to speak, lest any movement of the air cause the apparition to dissipate. He recovered his sense in time to drop behind a bush as the girl reared back on her heels, and her slim brown legs lifted her to standing. She stretched her arms overhead, lengthening her ribcage, and swayed her body side to side, luxuriating in the flexibility of her spine. She let her arms drop and twisted, smiling—until she saw Hoolow.

He tried to duck deeper behind the bush, but it was too late. She froze. He lifted his eyes, afraid to see her dematerialize, but she stood solidly before him. She took a cautious, curious step closer. His demeanor—kneeling, trying to cover himself with the bush—was a good indication of his harmlessness, but the sight of a man never seen before was unheard of and yet—as she took another step closer she saw something she thought had faded from the repertoire of her senses: he had the unmistakable color of the tribe about him. She dropped into a squat to catch him at eye level. His eyes widened as her warm proximity seemed impossible, and then she screamed with fright. She fell back onto her buttocks and scrambled backwards using hands and feet together. She rolled herself to standing and ran off, calling a high blue note that sunk low.

PART THREE

HOOLOW GOT TO HIS FEET. So she recognized him. Still shaken, he stood unmoving. Should he have anticipated her fright? Anyone who stayed away from the tribe for so long must be presumed dead. But she too was dead. Had he stumbled upon the human spirit world?

He heard the footfalls of the entire tribe, recognizing a few, but they were so jumbled together he couldn't put faces to them until the tribe was arrayed before him in a tight group, every body pressed to the one next to it. They stood as a single unit in opposition to him, all shifting at once as each attempted to capture a better angle of his profile. The whispered tones, "hoolow, hoolow," bandied back and forth. Whether they were hoping for confirmation of his identity or the opposite, he could not tell. Probably they didn't know themselves. The old feeling of humiliation and difference came flooding back. Was he to be more of a curiosity than ever? He'd gotten used to living alone, so comfortable with his own company he'd forgotten how it felt to be an oddity for others. The knowledge that all of his glaring inner reflection had resulted in no more than this compressed replaying of his earliest experiences was hard to bear. It wasn't different from what he'd expected, but the experience of it was much worse. Could he have prepared himself any better? How could he have known it would feel like this, and what now was the appropriate act? Should he throw himself to the ground at their feet and beg for acceptance? Had they even the capacity to give it? Perhaps they would pummel him into the dirt. Of course, they must think he was returning from the dead, as none of their kind had ever returned from such an absence. What else could they think? He pinched the flesh on his side and pulled at it so that they could see it snap back with life. They looked on as if their eyes were only facets of an individual, like the spots on a leopard. He thumped his hand on his chest in time to his heartbeats, and getting no reaction, had to drop his head to compose himself. It was not only his thoughts that were different; he must now convince them that his flesh was the same as theirs. Hopelessness loomed. He thought to turn away, but he wanted to absorb the beloved faces before him. Tentatively, he raised his eyes and searched out individuals. There were young ones he'd never seen before. He recognized the faces of children in some of the men. He tried smiling at them, and the group moved back en masse. He hung his head. He should never have searched for them. He thought again of retreating, but the loneliness of the cave surged up, and he knew he could not go back before making a greater effort. He lifted his chin defiantly and scanned the group still eyeing him with mouths agape. He found the soft face of the girl's mother, now with deep lines funneling across her cheeks, and he remembered his last glimpse of her moving toward the fire in despair of her lost daughter. His own eyes softened, and he reached out his hands to offer her the comfort he'd denied her on that night long ago. With the extension of his arms, the tribe leapt backwards. Squeals of fright rang out. They seemed to signify for Hoolow that any further efforts would be futile. He dropped his hands, but he allowed his eyes to linger. He wanted to remember every one of their faces, even the ones he didn't recognize, the young ones; he paid particular attention to the girl, who stood in the front and returned his gaze. He could see now that she was not who he thought, but her younger sister, the one he'd imagined pushing the meat between her mother's lips that awful night, and as he examined her, he became convinced that she'd done it in just that way. Despite the tension that creased her face, he could see its softness, so like her sister's in every feature it was remarkable. So this would be his last sight of the tribe. He would accept it, but the pain that welled up as he turned away nearly caused his knees to buckle. His first step faltered, and he felt a hand on his elbow. "Hoolow." The voice came so thinly to his ear that he thought his synesthesia had returned. It could be no more than the turning of a leaf that suggested a voice from the past, but when he looked up, he saw that the frail man standing before him with his white beard hanging over his chest was his old protector, who opened his arms like featherless wings, exposing the hollow gaps between the ribs that had once rung with bellows. Hoolow flung himself into his embrace. The whitebeard laughed and slapped his back. Then the tribe surrounded him, touching him everywhere, saying, "hoolow, hoolow," even the little children who'd never seen him before, and with tears in his eyes, he lifted them and pressed their smooth, innocent faces with his cheek. "Yes, Hoolow," he said.

The once young hunter knelt beside his leg and drew a questioning finger over his scar. In a flash of pique, Hoolow said, "Rawr," and clawed the air. The tribe fell back from him in a moment of fright and then came forward again, patting his body as if consoling him for a fresh injury. He was moved by their tenderness, the feel of which he'd forgotten, and felt guilty for his impulsive exaggeration.

Snug in their new shelter, their singing enveloped him so that he felt like the child who had sat on his mother's lap, the blackbeard by her side. The same man, white with age, sat next to him now. Hoolow was overwhelmed by the feeling of cohesion within the group. He had not expected to feel immediately like an inextricable part of it.

The tribe's five adolescent members, three young men and two women, including the girl's sister, sat in a tight huddle at the back of the shelter. They leaned in close and whispered their conversation so the others in the tribe couldn't hear—and why should it matter if they heard or not? The elders appeared to ignore them and that in itself seemed strange to Hoolow. They were so accustomed to this odd behavior of their youth that they had stopped noticing it. He remembered each youngster as a child squealing with delight, and he wanted to get close to the one who looked so like her sister, but when he presumed to join their group, all smiles, they fell silent and looked surprised. He shared their discomfort but had no idea of the cause. He had interrupted something—what? He smiled and stood up, moved to a more welcoming huddle, and in a few moments he heard the whispering recommence. A funny sensation burned the back of his neck. He was certain he was the topic of their conversation—but why would that be? He hadn't been around long enough for them to find a reason to mock him. No, it's not mocking. He had the feeling of being analyzed. These kids were different from the others, but he was distracted from ruminating on the reasons why, when the girl's old mother stood up to dance. She'd grown fat in her remaining daughter's care. Her rolls rippled as she executed mesmerizing shimmies.

The men watched with erections, eyeing each other peripherally, trying to judge how quickly to stand when her dance was done, because they wanted to be the first without appearing too eager. She would not discriminate in her choice. She kept her eyes closed and laughed. When the formerly young hunter took her hand, she opened her eyes to see Hoolow still sitting, embarrassed, and she laughed harder. He was the same without a doubt.

Hoolow watched them walk out of the circle of light, but he was soon reabsorbed in the gyrations of the next dancer. It went on until he fell into an exhausted sleep, all the day's excitement weighing on him.

In the morning he woke alone and was at first frightened by thinking he'd only dreamed his reunion with the tribe. Sitting up, he saw all of their things scattered about and revised his presumption to abandonment. They didn't want him after all. Then he heard distant voices. He smelled the nuts roasting. The women were returning with the first morning shoots. The old whitebeard sat in the shadows and laughed at his relief. He'd slept through to daylight, and as this shelter was angled toward the setting sun, it was dark in the mornings. He sat with the women and the old man, enjoying the feeling of privilege the situation afforded him. His thoughts turned to the five youngsters. The young men were surely off hunting with the rest of the men, but where were the girls?

The whitebeard donned his sling and walked about the shelter, prodding the women with his foot, thus accusing them of laziness. They laughed and swatted his knees but soon rose to follow him as he led them on their rounds.

Hoolow reclined by the fire, full of satisfaction. He could see how the women adored the whitebeard. They would treat him like a special infant as they guided him on their secret trails, offering him the choicest morsels they came upon. When his sling was half full, they would prop him in the shade and weave pretty stones into his beard. When his desire for them expressed itself, they would satisfy him, and he would giggle and gurgled like a wise baby. It was nothing less than he deserved.

Hoolow headed toward the spring for a drink and was surprised to find all five of the young people gathered there. They fell silent as he approached. He smiled at each of them in turn. The boys lifted their lips but let them fall back into sullenness almost immediately. The sister smiled and turned her head away, while the last of them beamed and thrust out her chest. Every reaction seemed unnatural to him as he knelt for a drink. He stood and smiled at them again. This time even the boys looked away after a brief grimace. Hoolow left them, but when he could no longer feel their eyes on him, he concealed himself behind a boulder, hoping to overhear their conversation.

"Where has he been all this time?"

"Do you think hoolow knows anything about why we are different from the elders?"

"Can't you see he is just like the others? He barely speaks." This came from a young man, who leaned with one foot resting on the rocks behind him so that his knee jutted a dramatic angle.

"Give him time. Maybe he knows something he's not saying," said the young woman, who switched a twig from one cheek to the other with her tongue.

"Why keep it a secret?"

"Maybe he thinks we won't understand. Maybe he thinks we're just like the others," she replied.

The girl's sister did not speak.

Hoolow was struck—was it possible these youngsters had thoughts like his own? Here they were speculating to each other in the way he'd speculated to himself. They used words, "we" and "you," words he'd never heard before, and yet their meanings seemed clear. They were addressing themselves as well as each other. The difference must be evident to them as it was to him. What other explanation could there be? He kept his silence, waiting for a chance to contemplate.

Nipples chomped hard on her twig while she folded Jitters' hair into a single neat braid. Her own hair was a long black slick she refused to plait, because she said she liked the feel of it sweeping over the top of her buttocks. When she had finished with Jitters' hair, she sat back in the shade of the rock and sighed. Jitters reached out to stroke the locks she longed to twine. Nipples indulged her until Jitters' fingers began to separate the strands, then she shook her head, saying, "That's enough." She spit out her mangled twig and licked her lips. Jitters could see what kind of mood she was in. Her upper eyelids slunk down over the tops of her pupils, and she cooed in the boys' direction. "Oh, Hum, come here boy," she said. Hum was at her side in an instant. She went from sitting to kneeling and taking his penis in her mouth. Jitters, not knowing why she felt so uncomfortable, got up and walked away. Mole joined the engaged couple, knelt behind Nipples and moved her thick hair over her shoulder so he could smooth his hands down either side of her spine. In this position her lower back arched out her buttocks.

Nose watched and despite his excitement, there was another, deeper feeling. Although he'd like to join the trio, and had no doubt he'd be welcomed, he was reticent.

Something niggled him. Where had Jitters gone off to? Why did she always wander away when their activities turned sexual? If she would not participate, how could he?

When they had been small together, he'd once found her sitting next to the cairn that had appeared after her sister's death. He had wondered at her attraction to this place that smelled of death, a repellent to him and the others, and yet the tiny girl sat leaning against it, staring at the sky, removed from all the other tribemates of their age. Nipples and Mole and Hum, before they had names, were back at the spring, splashing in the pool that was waning into the dry season. They were absorbed in one another; he alone had wondered where the other girl had gone. Seeing her quiet repose stirred something in him. He realized something about himself—he was alone, too. It was a startling revelation. He ran to her, threw himself to the ground and embraced her, crying. She clung to him, bursting with her own sobs, and when the tears subsided, she held him back at arms' length. They stared into each other's eyes. Nose knew he would not really be alone as long as there was Jitters. She was the first to recognize him, he the first to recognize her, and seeing the tiny inseparable couple walking everywhere hand in hand, had sparked something in their companions. They looked at each other more closely, and it wasn't long before the distinctions between them seemed to grow more obvious and more endearing. Their nicknames sprung from a new sort of affection. Nose's large proboscis became huge, and they loved him for it. At first when they called him by it, it made their own noses feel small and distinct. Over time they forgot his name had any meaning other than "him." But Nose could not forget his special attachment to Jitters. He, like the others, had forgotten the origin of her name.

Nipples was moaning, and Nose crouched behind a rock. He told himself, I could join them if I wanted to, and he tried to conjure the curves of Nipples' newly sensuous body to go along with her pleasure shrieks, but the image was superseded by that of the little girl whom he once teased for being too skinny. Her narrow ribs puffed defiantly. He wanted Jitters. He could be patient, because he realized she was filled with as many thoughts as he was, and it was bound to be confusing, as confusing as his own reasons for not joining the other three when that was what he wanted. He thought of Jitters; he replayed his memories of her developing body—her breasts burgeoned, her hips swelled, and at each increment there was a pause when he'd tried to touch her and she'd flinched away.

Hoolow helped the women pile nuts onto the fire while they waited for the hunters. Hoolow anticipated feasting on the flesh of a large animal, freshly killed, like he hadn't tasted since he'd last been with the tribe, so he was disappointed when the hunters returned with a scant string of rabbits, game he could have captured himself. The women cooed over the catch as if it were calf's liver, but Hoolow was soon distracted by the hunters, who surrounded him and tilted the tips of their spears in his direction. Cold fear slid through his gut, and he nearly loosed his bowel on the shelter floor: they meant to kill him after all. The men laughed and shook their spears. The formerly young hunter made a couple of short jabs at Hoolow's chest before reaching out to tap his fingernail against his spearhead. The thin blade of chert vibrated, ringing throughout the shelter. Hoolow still did not understand. The formerly younger hunter stepped forward. He rested the butt of his spear on the floor so that its blade was before Hoolow's eyes. He rotated the shaft so that the blade turned in the bright evening sun streaming into the shelter. At its center, the spearhead was no wider than Hoolow's smallest finger. He ran his thumb over its face; it felt slick and faintly pocked like the skin of a snake. The blade glowed, so thin it was translucent at the edges. Hoolow had never seen anything so finely made. The others thrust their spearheads before his eyes, and he marveled at them one after another. "How?" he asked.

Just then the five youngsters came into view as they made their way up the path to the shelter. The hunters pointed to the three boys walking behind the two girls. Hoolow gaped. Those youngsters were responsible for this? He looked back at the spear he held in his hand.

The rabbits' fat dropped onto the fire and permeated the shelter with its rich smell. The people began to gather around, except for the five youngsters who segregated themselves in the back. Hoolow positioned himself with his back to the youngsters, but within easy hearing distance.

The first carcass was broken apart and its best pieces passed to Hoolow, who accepted graciously. As he tucked into a pink haunch, he was astonished to see the old mother carry a portion to the youngsters before resetting herself next to the flames. Hoolow had never seen such preferential treatment of ones so young. The hunters, just as Hoolow remembered, refused any portion of the meat, patting their bellies and repeating, "full, full" to the women, who snickered and chided them but not too persistently as they were eager to consume what remained of the meat themselves.

Hoolow watched the familiar play with satisfaction while he kept an ear trained to the conversation of the youngsters. There was much lip-smacking and the repetition of familiar words—nose, nipples—at odd places in their discourse. Hoolow struggled to make sense of what he was hearing without giving any hint of his distraction to those around the fire. His attention remained divided even once the singing had begun.

One of the young men stood and walked to the edge of the shelter. Hoolow followed him with his eyes. It was dark now, the only light supplied by the fire. From the waist down the boy was illuminated, and Hoolow's eyes were drawn to a dark spot on the boy's left buttock. It was slightly raised and the size of a thumbprint. One of the girls called out, "Mole." The boy turned as if he'd just heard someone make his call. "Don't forget to use the leaves." Laughter erupted from the youngsters; it was accompanied by a loud fart, and as the stench reached Hoolow's nostrils, the spot on the boy's buttock again came into view. Mole, thought Hoolow, Mole.

In the morning the hunters pestered him to join their party. He refused, having no more liking for hunting than before his self-imposed banishment. They tried to entice him with their shapely new spear points. He made a show of admiring their craftsmanship, but even as he did so, his eyes followed the pack of youngsters drifting away from the rest of the group. They looked wary of being followed, although no one in the tribe, man or woman, paid them any attention. He noted the direction they had taken before tagging after the women, intending to question them as to the nature of their nearly adult offspring.

At first he was unaware of the women's discomfort with his presence. They were determined to tolerate him because of the possibility that he had returned from the dead and should be given his way lest he exert some power over them that they couldn't imagine. The whitebeard was the only carefree one among them. He stalked through the grass alongside the trail and scanned the horizon as if searching for prey. As he leaned into a squint, the lion's tooth, still hanging from a tattered thong around his neck, flapped forward and back against the dry skin of his chest. When he looked at the ground, he hooed with delight and tore at the plants, stuffing them into his sling. He danced to another tuft of coarse grass and with equal delight, tore at the sharp blades, oblivious to the tiny cuts they left on his palms. Hoolow would have liked to help with the gathering, but remembering their ways, he restrained himself. It was easy to look detached, because his thoughts were elsewhere, wondering what the youngsters were up to. He asked the old mother, "Why doesn't the daughter help?"

Her mother pursed her lips and turned her head away.

Hoolow persisted, "Where do the young ones go?"

"Don't know," said the old mother and moved away from him.

The diffidence of her response made him shy. Obviously her daughter's behavior was as much a mystery to her as it was to him. He noticed that all of the women had their backs to him, and he realized he was not welcome. He went in search of the youth.

He tracked their footprints in the sand, recognizing the five overlapping pairs, male and female together, which was unusual for people their age.

It wasn't long before he discovered four of the youths gathered beneath a tree. The girl's sister rested her back against its trunk. Although he'd struggled for it the night before, he hadn't been able to figure out her name. The one they called Nipples lay with her head in the sister's lap. Mole and the unnamed boy sat to the sister's right. Nose—his name was right there on his face—stood before them. He moved his body as if acting out a dream, and this was not so different from scenes Hoolow remembered from his youth. He drew closer, straining to hear.

"So, this one dog breaks away from the pack." Nose crouched and trotted. The ones beneath the tree watched with only mild interest. Nose stood and looked around at the ground. "Look," he said, "Say this rock here is the goat." He bent and with some effort, turned a heavy rock on its side. He scooped smaller rocks around its base to hold it upright.

The others grew attentive. Nipples rolled to her side and sat up.

Nose picked up a handful of pebbles. "The dogs tracked it." Nose walked a few paces, letting the pebbles dribble from his palm as he went, making a rocky trail on top of the dirt. "Until they found it on this rock outcrop." Nose knelt in the dirt a second time. He pushed some smaller rocks into a pile and set an ovoid-shaped cobble upright at its apex.

Mole stood and walked to the first rock Nose had set up. "Let me get this straight," he said. "This rock here is the goat."

"Yes," said Nose. The ones under the tree nodded, agreeing.

Mole walked along the path of pebbles, pointing down at it as he went, "These show where the dogs tracked the goat."

"Yes, yes," said Nose. He moved his hands to his hips and tapped one foot impatiently.

"This rock here is also the goat, but these other rocks she's standing on are just rocks."

The ones under the tree rolled with laughter. The other boy slapped the ground.

Mole looked back at them over his shoulder, a bemused smile on his face.

Nose brought his arms across his chest, his face red.

Mole looked down at the rock standing upright on its little pile. He scratched behind his ear. Then he asked, "How did she get so much smaller?"

The laughs under the tree shook the leaves.

Nose threw up his hands and stormed away.

"Aw, come on, Nose," called Mole between guffaws.

The other boy cupped his hands around his mouth, "You didn't tell us how the dogs tracked her over the rocks!"

The girls were too broken up to speak. Nipples wiped tears from her eyes.

Hoolow clapped his hand over his mouth, so that the laughter gurgled in his belly.

As Nose approached the shelter that night, he saw that the other youths sat about the fire, mingled amongst the elders. He took satisfaction in this, thinking, without me they have no focal point. Hoolow sat on the far side of the circle. Nose stepped up next to Nipples, who scooted over to make room for him; he dropped down beside her. The others had already begun their monotonous singing, but Nipples handed him a choice piece of meat. She'd held it pressed between her calf and thigh as she sat cross-legged, so it was free from dirt. Nose accepted it with gratitude. The exasperation he'd had with his fellows earlier in the day melted away as he sucked on the meat. He worked a morsel between his teeth and glanced around at the others. Mole and Hum both met his eyes with questioning looks. Nose shrugged and tilted his head to the side, meaning all was forgiven, and the faces of the other two brightened with relief. He was savoring the meat, chewing to the beat of the song that flowed through the shelter, when he felt Nipples fidgeting next to him. He turned his half-closed eyes in her direction and saw that her mouth was fixed in a sort of flirtatious moue. He followed her gaze across the fire to where it landed on Hoolow. Nose swallowed, and the masticated glob on his tongue found the opening of his throat. He choked and pounded his chest with the side of his fist. The elder woman sitting to his left slapped his back, but Nipples barely flinched. The meat dislodged and settled back in his cheek for further chewing. Nose tossed his female elder a look of thanks. Her hand settled on his inner thigh. Ignoring it, Nose looked subtly back to Nipples. One of her eyelids came down in an exaggerated wink. Nose's eyes flashed over to Hoolow, just in time to see a surprised look cross his features before he looked away. Nose dropped his gaze. He stared at the fire, confused, no longer tasting the meat. He looked again at Nipples. She held her lips between her teeth and was biting down hard, hard enough to bring tears to her eyes. Why did she want Hoolow? The hand on his thigh gave a squeeze, and he jumped. The old woman laughed. Nose met her eyes, but then stared back at the fire. She shifted her attention to the man sitting on her other side. Nose thought, why would Hoolow refuse such an invitation from Nipples? He recalled Hoolow's long stare at Jitters on the day she'd discovered him by the spring. Like me, Nose thought, he prefers Jitters. The thought troubled him. Why would Hoolow have such a preference? Nipples was just as comely as Jitters and no older. He felt Nipples leave his side. She walked halfway around the circle of humans before placing her hand on the shoulder of one of the older men. He rose without hesitation, and Nose watched them walk from the shelter.

Nipples returned with her chest held high. She'd done her one time lover a favor, and Nose knew that her posturing was meant to reassure the other youth that she really belonged with them. Nose had never gone with her, thinking her a bit dim. When his need was great, he sometimes went with a non-thinking woman, but he always thought of Jitters. Her body was the full, rounded body of a woman and not a girl's lithe form, yet she had never conceived. Jitters went with no one. It made her something of an oddity to the rest of the tribe, but Nose knew that when Jitters did choose, she would choose a thinking man, and despite what some of the others thought, Nipples in particular, he was convinced that there were only three in this tribe; however, he wanted the competition to be well defined, and not, he told himself, because he wasn't confident, but because Hoolow was bigger, a full-grown man who was thought to have conquered death. Nose would not be able to best him physically. His superior thinking ability was the advantage he meant to play.

A full cycle of the moon had passed since he'd rejoined the tribe, and Hoolow continued to track the youth. On this day their traces revealed a further deviation from the norm: they ground their heels into the dirt as if marking their trail for him to see. On previous occasions, when he was still far behind, they had spoken loudly to each other. They pretended they did not know he was there, but he suspected them of waiting for him to catch up when he fell behind. He had not heard his call spoken since the first day he'd come upon them at the spring, so he could not be certain of their interest in him. He continued to conceal himself from their view, understanding that they preferred each other's company because of the peculiar way they conversed with one another.

He had managed to figure out the names he had missed earlier. The boy was called Hum, and the sister: she was Jitters. This realization gave him immense satisfaction, but he kept it to himself. The youngsters' names were a secret code they liked to bandy about the shelter. Their elders had never figured it out. Were Hoolow to reveal his knowledge, the youngsters would know that he was like them. He might reveal himself only to be rejected, and where would that leave him? An outsider again. He would still be a member of the larger group, but already they were starting to bore him as they had in the past, and he noticed that the kids, too, were bored. They were not content to sit around the fire and intone the same old meandering tunes night after night. Recently he'd heard Nipples comment, "It drives me mad!" She emphasized the words with her expression and without raising her voice for the ones outside their tight clutch to hear, but Hoolow's ear was trained to their whispers.

The others had nodded their heads in agreement, and Hoolow sympathized. It was getting harder to concentrate on the songs, and he envied the youths their ability to entertain each other with conversation.

He remembered the bold look Nipples had tossed to him across the fire, her lips puckered as if kissing the air. At the time he was embarrassed to discover that he was intimidated by her. He figured that she had thoughts something like his own. What would she be thinking during the act of lovemaking?

Nose waited until he heard Hoolow scuffling behind a nearby rock. Then he turned to the girls. "You see," he explained with enthusiasm, "you can throw farther if your arm is longer. It makes sense, right?"

The girls nodded their heads, Jitters feigning a bit more interest than Nipples, who was having one of those moments when her chronic stick-chewing seemed to absorb all of her attention.

"You see here how we hollowed out the end of the spear?" Mole was most enthusiastic about this feature, it being his sole contribution to the design.

"It fits over this prong here." Nose held up the atlatl for their closer inspection.

Jitters nodded again; Nipples chewed her stick.

"So you hold it up next to your ear like this." Nose demonstrated, the atlatl resting in his palm, his index finger looped over the spear shaft to steady it. "Now you're ready to throw," he said, took three running steps and flung the atlatl forward with all his might. The spear hurtled through the air until it was almost out of sight. The girls shrieked with delight, and although the boys had seen it before, had practiced it for hours to get it right, they cheered just as loud. From his perch behind the rock, Hoolow gasped; he'd stood to see how far the spear flew and so he was exposed. He dropped back to his knees before any of the others turned.

"My turn, my turn," said Mole, dancing up to Nose with a new shaft at the ready. He fitted its hollow butt to the atlatl prong and took his stance for the girls. He looked over his shoulder to make sure they were watching, and this time they were intent. Mole exaggerated his pose before taking his running paces. His release was not as smooth as Nose's; the shaft wobbled in its flight and fell short of the first toss, but it didn't matter. The girls cheered, thrilled by a demonstration of power that appeared super human. They'd never seen a spear travel so far. No one had. Hoolow, too, was in awe, but rather than focusing on the rippling muscles of Hum as he stepped up to take his turn, he examined the mechanism. It was easy to see how it worked—it made the throwing arm longer. Its obviousness seemed comical to him. How had no one ever thought of this before?

Hoolow was brought back to the scene before him by Nose, who was shaking the atlatl in the air, chanting, "Ooga booga, ooga booga." He shook the atlatl at the others, saying, "Like monkeys! They do everything the same way over and over. If not for us they'd be using the same old points. Never anything new for them. They don't know the meaning of 'I.' Do you, hoo-low?" He hooed the descending tone derisively.

Hoolow blinked. Had he heard right? Was he being addressed?

Nose stalked to the rock behind which Hoolow was hiding. Hoolow stood to face his interlocutor and the rest, who hung back although keen on his response.

"Oh, I'm sorry," Nose mocked, "You don't know what 'you' means do *you*?" His laughter was cutting. "Hooo-loow," he hissed so that the tones were barely recognizable. "You don't have a proper name, because you don't know what a name is, man from the dead. Man from the dead, I think you've just been lost. Isn't that right? You just found your way back." He puckered his lips and diddled them with the side of his finger. The gesture was calculated to make the girls laugh, and they could not help themselves. Mole and Hum joined in with raspberries.

Nose watched Hoolow turn away. He was well satisfied with the evidence before him: if Hoolow were a true thinking man, he would not have allowed himself to be denigrated in front of the girls. He would have spoken up and put an end to the mockery. At the least Hoolow was weak.

Hoolow walked away from their jeers, secure in his secret knowledge. Although he longed to reveal himself, he would not be goaded into such a momentous step. What Nose asked, or rather the other, interior self that allowed him to ask it, was the very thing Hoolow had come to renounce. Could he revise his decision because of a new and surprising circumstance? It was a thing he'd never thought possible: others like himself. But he'd struggled learning to repudiate that inner self that longed for just the kind of individual attention now available to him. Its allure felt inescapable. But he could not let his time alone be for nothing. The youngsters indulged one another's thoughts. He could see that. They created new thoughts just to amuse each other.

What if he were to engage with them? New thoughts would breed uncontrolled in his head. He'd worked hard to escape that condition. It was fascinating to observe the youngsters, but did he want to be one of them? He'd passed that stage of his life alone, and he looked back on it with pangs of regret, but it could not have been helped. There were no others like himself then. But here they were now—could he not make up for the experience lost to him in his youth? How he had longed for such conversation in those times! He had wanted understanding, and now he could have it with these new ones. At what cost to himself? He'd sacrificed much of his inner self to be a member of the larger group. They were in awe of him. They gave him the best pieces of meat, although he did not hunt the larger game with the men. He slept by their sides at night, and their warmth had never meant more to him. Consorting with the youngsters would distance himself once again. But he could be a part of a new group. He could be a mentor to them. The last thought was ludicrous. It seemed he had much more to learn from the youth: about community, about conversation, about how their thoughts worked together, when his had always been singular.

Jitters and Nipples lay on their backs, head to foot, atop a flat, luxuriantly smooth rock. Jitters let her arm flop over the side, her fingertips dipping into the warm brackish pool at the bottom of which was the special white clay the women favored. The sun was high in the sky, and Jitters stared up at it behind her closed eyelids. The red disk pulsed, but it was not enough. She squeezed her eyelids tight, and a few gold sparks flitted across her field of vision before winking out. Seeing Hoolow that first day by the spring had been a shock. She still felt herself reeling from the sight of the tribe's brilliant color surrounding him, an aura she couldn't recall seeing since early childhood. She'd nearly forgotten what the colors looked like; she'd been consumed with thoughts, especially when it came to evading Nose's ever more frequent looks of desire, which she didn't share. He wanted too much of her. It seemed wrong to Jitters for anyone to know every part of her—the way she knew Nose. His inventiveness was charming, but it seemed more a quirk than a source of attraction. He was too familiar: from his hammertoes to his plump earlobes there didn't seem to be anything to discover about him. Why couldn't she be like Nipples? When Nipples wanted satisfaction from the boys, she commanded and they complied. Jitters wondered if she used the same commands, would their responses be the same? But she realized this was not what she wanted. She wanted to be like Nipples in wanting the boys to do what they did for her. She did not have the same desire. She felt about Nose the way she would feel about her mother's son. None of the others was any more attractive to her, but now there was Hoolow—that unmistakable aura, at once recognizable at the same time a thrilling surprise! It was gone by the time she returned with the rest of the tribe, and she hadn't seen it since. She spread her legs so that the sun beat down on her newly furred pubis. She smiled to herself, listening to the children running through the grass. When one hit a bramble there was a dry crackle accompanied by squeals of pain, then giggles and more of the tall blades wisping against each other.

Jitters heard a pair of splashes, then two more, and the water level crept to her palm. Nipples raised herself on her elbows. "They're here," she said.

A few flecks of water touched Jitters' cheek, and she opened her eyes. Her mother's smiling face hung over her. Jitters sat up and swung her legs over the side of the rock, so that her lower legs dangled in the water. The other women stood in the pool, pumping their knees up and down, kneading the clay with their toes until the pool turned to a thick white soup. The old mother reached below the surface and brought up a handful of white clay. She plopped it on the rock between Jitters and Nipples and pulled herself out to sit beside her daughter.

Jitters plunged a fingertip into the warm pile of clay, and steadying her mother's face with a hand below her chin, drew a line across the bridge of her nose. She leaned back to contemplate her next mark; her mother's broad smile was infectious.

Jitters glanced over to see Nipples working over her first subject, who sat with her back to her. Nipples stroked handfuls of clay into the thick ropes of hair. Her technique was aggressive, and her subject's head rocked from side to side under her manipulations. Nipples' expression started out fierce but softened as she sculpted downward turning horns and twisted spires. Her designs were not beautiful, but eccentric. When she finished with one, she shoved the woman from the rock and gestured for the next to take her place. The freshly coiffured staggered away in a daze, gingerly exploring the reconfigured terrain of her head with her hands. When there was a congregation of women whose heads were covered in horns and spikes, they searched each others' eyes for signs of their hairdos' effects. The giggles began, and Nipples and Jitters joined in.

Jitters found more excitement in watching Nipples performing her duties than she did in drawing her own designs. She'd become bored by decorating the bodies of the other women, only occasionally finding a flash of inspiration in an oddly cocked shoulder blade, but Nipples, as ever, seemed to be absorbed by her work, although afterward she would complain about it as she did about the singing, the irony being that of all the youth, Nipples was the best singer. Why would she deny her pleasure in it? Jitters sometimes suspected that Nipples "saw" more than she let on. She had been the last of their set to begin peppering her speech with the new words, "I" and "you." And at times like this, when she and Nipples were alone with the women and children, Nipples' face often fell into the sort of dreamy expression Jitters felt she herself only mimicked. Jitters thought of herself as "caught" between her mother's generation and their way of seeing and that of her peers, whereas Nipples appeared to glide between the two groups.

With all of the women decorated, the children emerged from the tall grass to gawk. The old mother shook her new collection of spikes at them. At first the children jumped back, but then fell to the ground and kicked their feet with laughter. One little one pointed to where the whitebeard was sleeping beneath a tree.

Jitters and Nipples watched from their vantage on the rock as the women and children gathered around the sleeping whitebeard. One of the children poked him with a stick until he rolled to sitting, flailing his arm against the irritant. When he opened his eyes, he let out a yelp of fright; then peals of laughter screamed out of him. The women and children laughed more, but this time, Jitters and Nipples remained unmoved. The joke had been worn out for them. They slid from the rock and went to search for the boys.

Despite his internal protestations, Hoolow remained drawn to the youth and continued to stalk them, overhearing conversations when he could. He did not always find them all together. Sometimes it was only the three boys.

"Where'd you get that?"

"I pulled it out of the lion's mouth."

The others looked at Nose skeptically, but it was not so far from true. If they were to believe their elders, the whitebeard was once a lion, and Nose had lifted the tooth from around his neck, while he was awake, no less. The old man had only smiled, as if he wanted him to have it. Nose would be the next lion. "Rawr," he growled as he swayed the tooth on its leather thong. "Rawr," he hissed and raked his fingers through the air, but it was an unconvincing performance.

"I'm the lion now," said Nose. He plunged the yellow tooth into his thigh and dragged it across his flesh. His eyes transfixed on the blood that oozed to the surface and trickled from the bottom of the laceration. It bent around his kneecap and cooled to the temperature of the air as it slid over his shinbone, sending a shiver of excitement through his body. The others watched him. He looked up with a smirk and struck blindly into his flesh a second time, tearing a gash parallel to the first. A quick glance confirmed a fresh red spillage, and he added another. Two more and he frothed with snarls. The others cowered in front of him. He was the lion. He had no mane, but his leg muscles twitched beneath the marks of his claws. The other boys fell to their hands and knees.

Hoolow watched the tooth passed hand to hand as the new initiates took turns inflicting themselves with similar wounds. He saw what they couldn't see—they were desperate for visions. They reacted to the bright color of blood. They needed it, were intoxicated by it, because all the bright colors of childhood that had abandoned them only recently were still vivid in their memories, but they were distracted by thoughts as he had been. Could the visions be a stepping stone to peace? This was not what his experience had shown him.

Hoolow knew the way to make the visions come, but he'd come to discount them in his time alone. Then again, even that peace he'd acquired through listening to his breath had been disrupted by his longing for the tribe. How could he watch these young people mutilate themselves without intervening? A temporary peace was better than none. He could guide them, show them the way to the visions, and with him there, they would not have to struggle through wrong interpretations as he had done. But it was something he had turned his back on. He reminded himself of the beauty of his visions. They would be so easy to recall.

As he walked, he saw a dark depression in the rockface above him. It was the type of cave required for visions. Although he had to scrabble over rocks, it was not too difficult. A path could be made. He crawled in to think. A few glowing threads cruised into his field of sight and wove together a harlequin lattice of luminous green. It throbbed in time with his modulated breaths. Yes, he could control the visions and help guide the others. He would be to them what he never had. But it was possible the others would not be able to see anything at all. They were caught up in each other's company in a way he never had been. He relaxed and let the visions envelope him, obliterating every sense but his eyes that twitched in his head, frantic to take in as much of the vividly swirling colors as they could. The visions had been this beautiful before, but he'd forgotten the impact of such beauty. He crawled out of the cave, euphoric and exhausted. What would the others think of it? He would be there to guide them so they didn't get confused as he had. It would be a step on a longer path to peace from the thoughts that must be torturing each of these youngsters as he'd been tortured. He only needed to stay alert to guide them.

Hoolow considered his new acceptance by the rest of the tribe, how he now sat within their midst and laughed when they laughed. Was this any different from how it had been before? He had changed, not them, although the new reverence they had for him had begun to wear off, and that afternoon, as he listened to the hunters tell of their latest success with the atlatl, he was as bored as he had been as a boy. They demonstrated the stance he'd already seen taken by the boys, and they did it with grace—because the principle of the thing was so simple. They took to it instinctively, but they'd no idea of how it had come about. It was magic to them, and as Hoolow listened to their bold descriptions of the hunt, he couldn't help thinking of the youth and marveling at their ingenuity. He felt certain that the sticks they carved for atlatls had not spoken to them. They'd received no directions for the making of such objects but had reasoned out their construction. It was a new concept. These hunters would not wonder at it, believing the youngsters' heard other voices. The hunters could not conceive of the kind of creative reasoning that had produced the atlatls, because the voices they heard spoke the same things.

The women sang out as they approached the shelter. The whitebeard walked at the back of their ranks, but when the women saw the men turn to greet them, they stepped aside so the whitebeard moved in front. His appearance was clownish—his head covered with grass sticking up in every direction, his cheeks smeared with ordinary brown mud, and his body covered with the swirling designs the women used to accentuate their curves, all done in the crudest manner, applied as a child might apply it. Hoolow was aghast, but the other men burst with laughter. For several seconds the old man was befuddled. His eyes combed the shelter for the source of their amusement, and seeing nothing out of the ordinary, he joined in their laughter anyway.

"Pretty, pretty," said the old mother, and she grabbed onto the whitebeard's shoulder to steady herself as she doubled up with laughter.

"Pretty, pretty," parroted the whitebeard, laughing as hard as the rest.

Hoolow was infuriated; the whitebeard's humiliation was intolerable to him. "Stop it! Stop it!" he shouted, stepping in front of the old man as if to shield him from their mirth.

"Hoolow, hoolow," said the whitebeard, slapping his thigh.

The others reacted with louder guffaws. Hoolow grasped the old mother's wrist and broke her connection with the whitebeard's shoulder. He flung her hand back down to her side, where it dangled as she looked up at him, hurt and bewildered. The others fell silent. Only the whitebeard continued laughing.

"Shame," said Hoolow, whirling his pointing finger in a gesture they all understood. "Shame on all of *you*," he said, confusing them with a word they only heard from their youth and didn't understand.

Hoolow took the whitebeard's elbow and led him away from the shelter. The whitebeard giggled in his grip, saying, "Pretty, pretty."

But Hoolow was still angered. He turned to glare at the old man and told him, "No, not pretty." He guided him toward the spring. The whitebeard followed solemnly, making Hoolow feel guilty for the harshness of his reprimand, but he still simmered with anger at the rest of the tribe. They had made an object of ridicule of a man Hoolow loved, and he could not easily forgive them. He had not been a witness to the slow waning of the whitebeard's strength. The image of him at the peak of his powers was fixed in his mind, and he could still feel the hands that had hoisted him into the air when he was a child. He knelt by the spring and reached up to take the old man's hand. It took some seconds for the whitebeard to lower himself. He stretched his legs toward the water. Hoolow scooped handfuls and splashed his thighs, rubbing at the mud where it stuck to his skin in clumps. The whitebeard helped, smearing out the lines on his chest. When Hoolow got to his face, the whitebeard held his head still. He stared at Hoolow, who focused on his work and avoided his eyes. When the old man's face was clean, Hoolow turned away and dipped his hands into the spring. The dirt clouded around his wrists, and he watched it swirl out into the water. He felt the whitebeard's stiff, damp fingers cup his jaw. He turned his head, reluctant to meet the whitebeard's gaze now that he'd time to regret the sharpness of his reaction. The whitebeard's mouth was grim. His eyes were weak, so he drew Hoolow's face close. "Hoolow, pretty," he said emphatically and threw back his head with laughter. To his surprise, Hoolow felt a chuckle emerge into his throat. The whitebeard held his sides. Hoolow managed a full laugh. He stayed sitting as the whitebeard got to his feet. He allowed the whitebeard to walk back to the shelter alone; he sat by the spring as the mud settled and his reflection began to appear on the surface of the water. He would be old sometime too, he thought. He would be old with no more purpose than to serve as a source for jocularity to those who were now young. He could hear their taunts: throwback—thought-less old man— never an independent idea in his head! Unlike the whitebeard, he knew he would never be able laugh at his own disgrace. He had to make himself known to them while he still could.

He called to him, "Nose."

The boy stopped cold with shock; his wide eyes narrowed in Hoolow's direction. Hoolow took pleasure in seeing him struggle not to let his panic show. "Hoolow," Nose said lowly and then looked away, embarrassed. His thoughts turned to confusion when Hoolow nodded and turned away.

Hoolow went about his business, but a bright flame flickered in his gut. So now he knows, he thought of Nose. I revealed myself to him. We've recognized each other. For the first time in his life, Hoolow felt the sweet burn of mutual understanding. It gnawed at him, begging for more fodder. What else might they come to understand of one another? What possibilities for shared experiences of which he was still incapable with the elders! His thoughts turned to Jitters, the way her eyes shifted away from him whenever he approached, but he knew that if he said her name, out loud, she would have to look. She would have to see him. They would see each other. He had the key. Would he use it? Could he resist?

He repeated her name to himself until it beat with its own repetitious life—Jitters, Jitters—it sounded in his ears with no prompting until he saw her, alone by the spring, and the refrain stopped dead. His head became hollow, no more than a bone shell to his lifeless brain. They exchanged shy looks, but as she walked away, the distraction of her swaying hips allowed his lips to find the word—"Jitters"—uttered with barely any breath, but she heard. He saw her stop and thought, what have I done? She turned, and her gaze fell into his. "Hoolow," she said and flicked her eyes away only to bring them back. They glared until he repeated—"Jitters"— louder this time, and she ducked her head, smiling to herself. She lifted a hand to try to hide her stretched lips and threw him a last glance up through her eyelashes before turning and sprinting away.

Hoolow sat down stunned. What had just happened? There was a connection, yes, but why had she broken it off when it pleased her? She acted as if frightened. As if she felt as he did, for his heart was pounding enough to make him dizzy—and what was that if not fright? But there was something more intriguing in this state. It stimulated no impetus to flee, rather he wished to pursue—but how? Did she want capture? Cajoling, perhaps? The appropriate action seemed impossibly obscured. It was something outside the scope of his knowledge. He got up dumbfounded.

As he stepped into their midst, they all looked at him expectantly. Jitters nodded encouragement, and he breathed in her strength. "I am like you," the unfamiliar words tripped over his tongue, but their significance made him choke back a sob the youngsters couldn't quite comprehend. They had no idea of the poignancy of this moment, having themselves always been surrounded by peers of their kind.

"Why don't you hunt with the other men?" he asked, eager to absorb himself in their conversation.

Nose spoke first, "We prefer to hunt on our own. We're much better at it. We make all of the tools for the tribe now."

"They have their own way of doing things and they don't like our suggestions," said Mole.

"We could be much better hunters than them," declared Hum. "But they won't let us."

"It scares them that we are so different, but they're happy to use our tools," said Nose.

"How do you make tools when the stones don't speak to you?" The new words still felt funny in his mouth, but he managed to speak them fluidly.

Nose shrugged, "The rocks do not speak to us the way they do to the older ones, yet we can make tools just as they do, only better." Then he laughed and added, "They say, 'The rock speaks clearly,'" and he mimicked the pointing gesture the rest of the tribe used.

"The rocks do not talk to me either," said Hoolow with delight.

That night around the fire everything was changed, although none of the members of the tribe outside of their immediate circle seem to notice it. They didn't intuit the switch in Hoolow's allegiance, and he felt like a traitor while exchanging knowing looks with the youngsters during the singing. They don't see the colors either, he thought, they are as distracted as I am. The rest go on singing with the same numb cohesion. Wasn't it lovely, though, the perfect harmony? It felt remote to him again. What felt near were the eyes of the young man sitting opposite him. They stared at each other across the flames in a way that bucked no threat. They shared their curiosity, each wondering what the other was thinking, Nose trembling inwardly as he presumed Hoolow's desire for retaliation against him, Hoolow too thrilled by his new association with the youth to remember any affront given him. Jitters surprised them both by getting up and taking Hoolow's hand to lead him away from the fire.

They walked a long way from the shelter, under the stars, holding hands. She stopped to gaze at the sky, and there was just enough light to see her closed lips pressed into a smile. Is this to be the place, he thought, here on the open ground with nothing to shield us from prying eyes? It seemed contrary to her shyness, but he was game nonetheless and began to orient his body to face hers, but she gave a little laugh and a tug at his hand, and they continued on. And on, so it seemed to Hoolow. If any children were following, they would have given up by now, and he chanced to worry. It's not safe for little ones so far from camp at night, and he cast a glance back over his shoulder. Jitters stopped again and looked back herself. "What is it?" she whispered, and he felt the fear shiver that traveled through her arm.

"Oh," he said, reminded of their purpose, "Nothing. It's nothing," and pretended he wasn't annoyed as he pulled her onward, urging her faster toward whatever far destination she intended.

They reached a large outcrop of boulders, and Hoolow stopped, out of breath with frustration. Apparently she had no place in mind as she'd taken to wandering by his side until he'd assumed the lead, not knowing whether it was appropriate or not. He felt she should make the first move. Had she made it so discreetly he hadn't recognized it? It seemed likely. She was so wonderfully shy. His tender feeling restored, he looked at her leaning against the rock, the moonlight creating a silver halation about her figure. Her face was in shadow, so he moved his lips to where he thought hers should be, and they stretched to greet him. The meeting of soft moist tissue promised more. His body reacted to this first taste by pressing her against the rock. She squirmed against the feeling of entrapment, causing Hoolow to think she shared his excitement. He reached to squeeze the fleshy part of her hip. She yelped and twisted. He stepped back, surprised, and she squirted away, leaving Hoolow to wonder if he'd stepped on her foot.

Flaccid and confused, he followed her back to the shelter, walking a few steps behind. She held her arms across her chest until they were nearly within the circle of light cast by the waning fire. Then she stopped, turned halfway toward him, waited for him to catch up, and even reached out to him so that they rejoined the tribe as they'd left it—hand in hand. She smiled at those around her and settled down to join in the singing. Hoolow sat by her side and mouthed to the rhythm of their song, too distracted by what had happened to attempt to sing in tune. She appeared unaffected by the encounter. Yet, he knew he'd done something wrong. Something he thought she'd wanted. She was a far more inscrutable creature than her sister ever was.

As the following day wore on, Jitters wished more and more to be alone so that she might contemplate her failed attempt at making love with Hoolow, but, as ever, she was afraid to wander too far from the rest of the tribe by herself. This had been her condition since the dissolution of her visions. To be alone without visions was to be too alone, adrift on a sea of anxiety, her eyes constantly scanning for predators, as she no longer saw their scent trails, and therefore suspected them of lurking behind every rock and tree. The sensation of being in peril was intensified when her thoughts inevitably dipped back to the scene of her sister's death. Her sister had been wandering far ahead of the other women, alone. The earlier events of that day were lost to memory— Jitters had been so small—but that one distant shriek could still pierce her. The women shouted and ran. Jitters stumbled as she tried to catch up, fearful for the first time of being left behind, and then came the picture of her sister's limp body in her wailing mother's arms. Too late.

Jitters shivered.

Nipples reclined in the cool shade at the back of the shelter where the ceiling was low. Jitters crawled toward her on hands and knees. She gained her side and sat back on her heels. "Do you want to do a little foraging? For ourselves? Just the two of us?"

Nipples spit out her twig but her mouth stayed open as if she were waiting for someone to stick in a new one for her.

Jitters felt that she was being studied, so she looked away.

"O-kay," Nipples drawled.

Jitters waited to be questioned. She sagged with relief when Nipples reached for her sling.

There was a trail used by the women early in the morning. Now, as the sun was beginning its descent, it was sure to be deserted. It was a narrow path, and Jitters walked in front. It was silly to think that Nipples' presence was all that was required to alleviate her fear, but it worked. On a good day, Nipples was a quiet companion.

As Jitters bent over an elderberry bush, she heard, "No, I don't like those, leave them there." Jitters, not really interested in gathering, was happy to move on, but the voice behind her was only beginning its litany of complaints: "Yeeck," "Not those," "Ouch!"

"Ouch," repeated until Jitters stopped and turned. Nipples stood on one foot while she massaged the sole of the other with her thumbs. Satisfied that there was no blood, Jitters kept her expression impassive. Nipples took the hint. "Stepped on a rock," she said apologetically, and Jitters continued down the path.

Finally she had some peace. At first she tried not to think, although that had been her purpose. A cool breeze whispered over her skin. If she could somehow get lost in that sensation she would not have to think, but the thoughts crashed in, and she couldn't avoid examining them. *What had me so scared? Certainly I felt safe again once we'd reached the rocks. Hoolow was there to protect me.* His lips were soft and inviting, absorbing, but then, so suddenly, the hard bulk of his body had pressed against her. It could only be that her fear was a too recent ember that flared at his hot breath on her neck. But it was Hoolow. He didn't mean her any harm, was incapable of it, and now must be confused by her behavior. She would remedy it, show him that she was not afraid of him.

"Ah, little help."

Jitters turned to see Nipples with her head bent back, her hair tangled in an overhanging branch. As Jitters unwound the shiny black strands, it became evident that Nipples had struggled before calling out, so she did not say what she was thinking: if you'd only let me braid it. . .

Hoolow said to the gathered youth, "I want to show you something in the deep cave. Something that will interest you."

"We are told never to go there."

"Disembodied animals are there."

"You will see," said Hoolow.

The others evinced no fear as they followed him up the path he'd created. Nose thought, is he showing us the source of his power?

Hoolow had already collected fagots for the fire in the cave entrance. They had to duck down to enter, but the space widened; it had a high vaulted ceiling that sloped toward a vertical crack they had to turn sideways to pass through. The crack opened into a smaller room, about a third of the size of the first. A narrower tunnel branched off to the left, one that required crawling on hands and knees, but they did not investigate this passageway.

Hoolow called them together in the dark, "Find a place to sit down and be comfortable."

They oriented themselves toward the sound of his voice and reached out their hands to either side, finding the hands of the others before sitting. The rocks on which they sat were damp, and the dirt clumped between their toes. The barest gray light flickered through the narrow opening into this room. If they looked toward the back they saw pure darkness. They felt their heartbeats and listened to their respirations as they were instructed by Hoolow, who hoped the visions would come on gradually, but Nipples began to croon a high pitched vowel, and the others joined in her song, their collective voice boosting its intensity until Hoolow, to his surprise, heard his own voice mingled with theirs. As he felt his throat contract to make the sound, the wavering shadow that draped the entryway tore from the wall and flashed about their heads. Jitters shrieked, and the now golden shadow reared back and pounded its forelegs in the air. The boys lowered the pitch of their chanting that seemed to have its own volition, summoning more and more animals to careen out of the crack and dash about the room, trailing illuminated dots that settled over everything. Another large fold in the rock wall created a deep undulating shadow. It leapt from the wall and galloped around their heads. Hoolow was shocked by the vitality of the beast. He'd examined his solitary visions quietly, so this was his first taste of how sound enlivened them. In their excitement, the pitch and speed of their singing increased, and more and more beasts jumped from the wall and circled round them, kicking up multicolored dust that infested the air with crepitating dots. The dots aligned themselves along their features, settling into the creases and filling the hollows around their eyes, so that their faces stood out in the darkness, illuminated in various hues. When the visionaries looked at their fellows, the dots coalesced to create auras to which they reacted with delight—their vision had been restored a thousand fold! They experimented with calling the visions forth, ululating the names of animals. When they sang fast, the animals charged around them, hooves dashing everywhere, causing no injury. When they slowed their singing, from tiredness alone, the animals stopped to graze, fading back into the wall as the visionaries drifted into sleep.

When they emerged into the daylight, the faces of the youth bore a euphoric blankness as if the visions had obliterated their unique qualities. Looking from one to the next, Hoolow realized he was seeing his own expression reflected and the recognition filled him with the most intriguing sensation. Before he could examine it, the youths' individual expressions returned. They wrapped themselves in their former identities as if it was the most natural thing in the world; they drew them out of the air. Walking back to the shelter they sang and skipped.

That night around the fire, they sat amongst their elders and the children, but it was as if they sat alone, each smiling across the flames at the others. Although each had never appeared more singular, Hoolow had never felt closer to them. He was filled with a sense of knowing, and thought, for the first time, these are my people. He chuckled to himself. The elder woman sitting next to him turned to him with a look of curiosity, the sort of look that had once caused him acute embarrassment. Now he thought, poor woman, she will never understand. She can never know what I have shared with these others, Nose and Nipples and Mole and Hum and Jitters. Hoolow looked across to Jitters and saw that her mouth was open and grinning, the skin around her eyes crinkling: she'd noticed the exchange with his neighbor. He looked around to the others of his set and saw that they also wore expressions of silent laughter. We are one, he thought with a charge of elation, sharing visions has made us one.

When he crawled to his depression in the back of the shelter, Jitters snuggled in next to him, her body warm and throbbing, but she rolled to her side and pushed her buttocks to his groin, unmindful of his erection. It was as though she were not present in her body. "Tomorrow," she murmured, "The cave. Tomorrow."

Yes, thought Hoolow, but he stopped himself from speaking aloud. Was it really such a good idea to take the youngsters back so soon? They'd taken to it much more easily than he'd thought, and the visions he experienced with them were so enticing, he'd lost track of his thoughts immediately. He had not been in control at all. I fancied myself a guide, perhaps no more than an observer standing by to buffet them back onto the right track should they bounce off of it, but I ended up a participant, as lost in the visions as any of the youth. My inner self dissolved into the others. Hoolow slept.

He awoke with a start. He lay still, trying to determine its cause, but the shelter was quiet, the elders and their children having gone on their rounds. Jitters had left his side. The youngsters sat about the fire's last embers, poking them with sticks.

"Finally," mumbled Hum as Hoolow crawled toward them.

Nipples pushed a pile of nuts in his direction.

He sat, eating silently, his thoughts constricted by the tension radiating off of his companions. He could not fathom it. Last night they were so happy.

"When may we return to the cave?" asked Nose. He watched Hoolow chew.

"Perhaps," he said and licked his teeth, "We should rest for a day. Too many visions can be wearying."

"We want to go now," said Mole.

Hoolow gazed around at their faces. Jitters' jaw was rigid. She looked away from him. He peeled another nut, pretending to be unmoved, but the meal in his gut soured. His abdomen tightened; its purpose seemed to be to root him to his place by the fire, peeling nuts, but at the same time his heart fluttered, urging him to action. Why not go to the cave? He waited for the answer while chewing another nut. He forced it down into his clashing innards. No answer came. He got to his feet and stretched. The others stared up at him. He shrugged and said, "Let's go to the cave."

"Really?" said Hum.

The others jumped to their feet. Nipples threw her arms around his neck. Jitters clasped his waist. The boys whooped, Nose already leading the way from the shelter. Hoolow laughed.

They sat in a circle as before, but gave no credence to Hoolow's instruction to listen to their breaths. Nipples began to sing with shaking confidence. The others joined her, already having figured out how to summon the visions. The air of the cave, which had been cool and clammy, became crisp. It crackled with the vibration of their singing. Hoolow's body felt like a vapor, its boundary defined by a sheen of sweat, his attention the only thing holding it together. As the intensity of the singing increased, he felt himself rise with the others, hands reaching out to caress the slick walls of the cave. Fingers made trails of wavy lines through the damp. The lines lifted and twisted into the shapes of the animals whose names they chanted—buck, bull, hare. When they were surrounded by the menagerie, their song reverted to tones—ah, oh, oo. Nose leaped up and threw his arms around the body of a buck, but it fell through his grasp and galloped into a shadow. Hoolow realized he was on his knees when Nipples climbed onto his back, reaching her hands toward the ceiling and gliding them over the rock; a flock of yellow finches rained over them. Two of the others pressed against Hoolow's sides, the rhythm of their breaths singing through their ribs. His eyes stayed fixed on his hands, their hands, hands moving this way and that over the rock. Mice, rabbits and squirrels scurried out of the waves, racing between his thighs and over his upturned insteps. The power he felt in their creation intoxicated.

As the other bodies fell away one by one, Hoolow's rose up. A thought appeared: what has happened? What happened to me? To my self? He looked around at the bodies lying about the floor of the cave. Nipples lay with her head resting in the curve of Jitters' side. Jitters' head moved up and down on Mole's belly. Mole's legs entwined with Hum's as if the pair had tripped over each other and slept where they fell. Hoolow looked for the last, Nose; he lay on the other side of the small cavern in front of the low passageway. He was on his side with his arms stretching out toward the others as if trying to draw them closer. Hoolow could not see his expression in the dark but could not help imagining it yearning, even in sleep. He is like me, like I was, he thought with pity, but then caught himself. He'd never before had such an experience as what he'd just shared with the youngsters. In retrospect it was frightening the way his thoughts had drained away taking his self with them. He had forgotten himself so quickly. The youngsters had taken their selves' disappearance in stride as here they all were sleeping peacefully. Of course, they hadn't the years of solitude and cultivation of selves that trembled in fear at the idea of dissolution. Hoolow's heartbeat quickened. He listened for the sound of his breath in the darkness. It took a few moments to distinguish his own breaths from those of the others, but once he found it, he was calmed. He lay back and allowed himself to sleep. When he awoke, the youths were ringed around, watching him. As his eyelids flickered up, they leaned forward. He saw how eager they were to question him, and he felt a tingle of authority that he wished to nurture. He didn't let on that he'd been as lost in the visions as they were but instead pretended expertise. Their natural confidence in him made the mantel of authority a light weight. He was willing to pontificate, and he spoke assuming they would understand concepts that had taken him countless moons to formulate, but these youngsters were so quick in all things. He didn't stop to consider their possible confusion. He answered their questions.

"What is this thing that produces all of our thoughts?"

Hoolow responded, "It is the animating energy that is in all things. All things contain this spirit," expecting them to easily grasp this idea. Was it any more complex than the atlatl?

"Do rabbits have spirit?"

"Yes."

"Do beetles have spirit?"

"Yes."

"Do rocks have spirit?"

"Yes."

"Trees?"

"Yes, yes, all things are imbued with spirit." Hoolow spoke of only one thing, but in the imaginations of the youngsters it was divided into many. Their thoughts had not undergone the tempering of much solitary reflection. After their collective visions in the cave, Hoolow's was hardly less brittle.

Scattered around the spring were many angular blocks of black basalt, and Mole and Hum reclined against one of them, shoulder to shoulder, each lost in contemplation. The rolling tumble of thoughts was something they'd never examined in themselves before, taking it for granted. Mole raised a hand to scratch above his ear, and the "skrtch, skrtch" so close to Hum's ear drew him out of his wonderment. He turned to Mole and asked, "If all things have spirit as Hoolow says, then why can we see the spirits in the cave but not all around us, all the time?"

"Because," said Mole, "outside the cave the spirits are contained in physical bodies that act as shields against our sight."

"Hm," said Hum, "what do you think is the substance of spirits? I mean, if they are separate from physical bodies, they can't be made of the same stuff, can they?"

Mole's eyes shifted to Hum. "I never thought of it before," he said, filled with new respect.

Hum felt the increase in his esteem and sat straighter. "And what," he exclaimed, "do the spirits of rocks look like? The spirits of animals look like animals, but we do not see the forms of rocks dashing about the cave!"

"Ah," said Mole, equally excited by the new topic of their conversation. He picked up a rock lying by the side of his foot and turned to face the basalt against which they'd been reclining. He scratched the rock across the black surface of the basalt, and it left a white mark. "Do you remember," he said as he added to the white streak, trying to shape it into a circle, "seeing a round shape like this? And it had lines coming off of it like this," and he added radials to his crude circle.

"Yes, yes," said Hum, taking up a small rock of his own, "and there were other shapes, long ones like this," and he drew an oblong shape and filled it with crisscrossed lines.

Mole was nodding, "There were many things with no shape floating about in the cave," and he drew a series of zigzagged lines.

At this moment the women of the tribe came to the spring to slake their thirst, but they were arrested by the red intensity of the voices of Mole and Hum. Their fervor sounded like anger to the women, who were frightened. The sight of Hum and Mole scrabbling on their hands and knees, facing the rocks, looked like a scene of madness, and swirling about the heads of the two boys were crazy abstract images that rotated and lifted off of the surfaces of the basalt. The women turned and ran. They retreated to the site of a ground spring, where, with much effort, they were able to squeeze a few muddy drops from the clay. It tasted bitter to them but must be better than the water of the fresh spring, which they assumed to be contaminated by a madness-causing substance, and how could that have happened?

"Hoolow," whispered one below her breath.

"Hoolow," whispered another.

That night, sitting around the fire, they confronted him. The old mother pointed at him, saying, "Brought sickness from the dead."

Hoolow was startled. The youngsters, who had been lost in their respective daydreams, grew attentive.

"At the spring there is the evidence."

The men, who'd been lounging at the shelter since mid-afternoon, were curious. As a body, they rose from their positions around the fire. The formerly young hunter took up a torch and led the way toward the spring; their footfalls sounded a purposeful chorus on the well worn path. The youngsters followed eagerly, the women trailing behind, and Hoolow bringing up the rear. He kept the pace in a sort of dreamy distraction, unable to imagine what had incited the women against him, but sure of his ability to explain it away, whatever it might be.

The man at the front held his torch high so that it cast a coruscating glow over the basalt, and the squiggling white lines Mole and Hum had drawn there during the day pulsed with life. The torch fell to the ground.

Hoolow heard the men gasp. They began falling back in front of him. The women ran as the youngsters pushed their way forward. Amidst the chaos, Hoolow raised the torch and was himself shocked by the white forms that jumped out of the darkness; he stepped up for a closer look. Behind him, Mole and Hum doubled up with laughter.

"What have you done?" Hoolow asked. He and the five youngsters were left alone at the spring.

"Look," said Hum as he ran to point out the different forms, "these are all shapes we've seen in the cave."

Hoolow appraised their handiwork. The shapes were suggestive. He could see what their intention had been, but the shadow of the rest of the tribe's uneasiness hung over the place. "This is dangerous," he said. "The rest of the tribe can't understand what we do in the dark cave. This is frightening to them."

"They're stupid," said Mole, and he crossed his arms over his chest.

Hoolow didn't know how to respond. The youth were hot to express themselves, but if this went on, it would cause further division within the group and that could not be good. "You have to make amends with them. Smooth things over."

Mole turned his face away. Nose and the two girls stepped up to the rocks. Hoolow watched as Jitters traced her finger over the outline of a circle. She turned to Hum and said, "It's wonderful." Hum beamed. Jealousy flashed through Hoolow's gut, but he managed to neutralize it with the memory of the last time he and Jitters were alone together, when she had smiled, picked up his hand and pressed it to the middle of her chest. He'd marveled, but when he attempted to probe her cleft, she pushed him away again. He had lain staring up at the stars, exasperated, while she snuggled against his side. He shook away the image and waved the torch back and forth in front of the drawings, causing them to dance. The youngsters "ahhhed." Hoolow could see the beauty of the drawings and was impressed. He reminded himself of his responsibility to these young people. He'd been the one to introduce them to the visions in the dark cave; the consequences, although unforeseen, were his to deal with.

"Listen," he said, "Can you find another place to do this? I know it's important to you, but don't do it here, at the spring, where the others will see it."

"What will we do about these?" asked Mole, resentfully.

Hoolow bent and scooped some of the mud from the edge of the spring. He smoothed it over the lines of Mole and Hum's drawings. The others grudgingly followed his example.

Hoolow began courting the women the next morning. Sensing their new distaste for him, he followed at a fair distance, but within their sight. He took note of the wary glances they cast in his direction and waited until they'd settled under a tree with the whitebeard before making his approach. The whitebeard grinned, but the women looked away. "Is there the smell of sickness here?" Hoolow asked, pointing to his chest and doing his best to present a soft expression. He went to his knees and extended his arm for them to sniff.

The whitebeard grabbed his hand and pressed his nose to his wrist; he inhaled with a dramatic snort and lifted his head, smiling. He held out Hoolow's arm for the women on either side of him. Reluctantly, they tilted their noses in its direction, but they did not smile their acceptance. They shrugged and refused to look at Hoolow, while the whitebeard nodded and beamed as if his ploy had been a complete success.

Hoolow got to his feet. "Come to the spring," he said, "It is safe now." He began walking in the direction of the spring. The women did not move. He motioned for them to follow and waited as they crossed their arms and shook their heads. The whitebeard struggled to his feet; the women watched as he shuffled after Hoolow, following when they realized they had no other choice.

The women dragged their feet and stopped to watch as Hoolow lifted up handfuls of water so the old man would not have to kneel. Beyond the pair they could see the basalt blocks smeared with brown mud, crackled in the sun. It was not as it should be but neither was it frightening. They approached the spring and drank of its clear water, but they still didn't smile at Hoolow. He realized he would have to make a much broader gesture.

He found the youngsters lounging around the opening of the dark cave, discussing their most recent visions. Mole and Hum were doodling on the rocks. He sat amongst them and spoke softly, "We have to do more to mollify the rest of the tribe."

"Shall we go into the cave?" asked Nipples. Her excitement was catching. The others looked to Hoolow, and he nodded. He followed them into the cave and sat among them as they began to sing. They had begun adding words to their songs. Nipples had been the first to do so, and the others picked up on her innovation. Hoolow waited to hear their ooos and ahhs in the dark, an indication of their absorption in the visions, before slipping away into the tight passage off to the left. At first he crawled and then slithered until both shoulders touched the walls of the passage, and he relaxed into its embrace. He tried to push the conflicting thoughts from his head. Had he done right by bringing the youths to the cave? It had driven the division in the tribe deeper. The close space magnified the sound of his breathing. There was no need to close his eyes. The soothing blue vapor enveloped him, and he remembered his days of solitude with nostalgia. How might he recapture that peace and make it felt by the rest of the tribe? If only he could go back in time and undo the offense. Mole and Hum had not given much weight to the desecration of the spring. They were unruly. Already they were making new designs on other rocks, and Hoolow only hoped the rest of the tribe would not discover them. He had no hope of controlling them. All the youngsters had leaped ahead of him in their ability to manipulate the visions with sound. He could hear them in the larger chamber. He felt warm; their voices crackled the bottoms of his feet, and he thought of fire. *Was* there a way to go back and erase the offense? He remembered the way the graybeard had danced over the flames; sparks flew in the air, sending the tribe into trance. If he could make the sparks mean something. If he could transfer Mole and Hum's offense to the sparks, then it would indeed dissipate in the air. Everyone would see it, and their misdeed would dissolve in the tribe's collective vision. All he needed to do was explain to the kids how it would work. If they agreed to participate, the others would believe what they saw. He rejoined them when their song began to slow, indicating they were winding down. Soon their visions grew stagnant, and they succumbed to exhaustion.

He introduced the new idea when they awoke, never realizing he'd been gone. "I've the solution. Here's what we'll do. . ."

Mole blew on the stick and handed it to Hum, who pursed his lips around a smile and exhaled loudly before passing the stick to Nose. Nose knew himself to be blameless, but he blew seriously. He understood what it meant to the other members of the tribe, who watched with rapt attention. Hoolow took the stick and said, "All that is not good is held within the stick. Watch it burn and disappear."

The tribe was riveted as he threw the stick onto the flames. It popped and twisted, turning to cinders, and the youth exchanged smug expressions as the rest of the tribe followed the sparks of their mistake spiraling up in smoke.

After a few moments passed, the formerly young hunter spoke, "This is good, but the youth must do more. All the points are broken now." He pointed at the three youngest men of the group. "Must make more."

Hum huffed and rolled his eyes. Hoolow saw his success threatened, and he drew the three young men aside. "Listen," he said, "just do this. How hard is it?"

"It means we'll have to give up time that we could spend doing things that we like," argued Mole.

Hoolow winced at his petulant tone. "For the good of the tribe," he said, "We have to all live together here. Let's make it as easy as we can."

"Who says we have to live together?" asked Hum.

Hoolow was stunned by the question.

"Why don't we take the girls and make our own tribe?"

"Split the tribe?"

"Why not?"

"Fools," said Nose, "You don't even want to make tools. You want to have to do all of your own hunting?"

"I don't mind," said Hum, puffing up his chest.

"With all of our innovations it would be a snap. Especially if we didn't have to worry about all of these others," added Mole.

Hoolow hadn't considered the possibility of splitting the tribe, and yet it was not an altogether distasteful idea to him. He could see how things could be made simpler, but for now he needed to focus their attention on the situation at hand. "It will not take you much time to make the points for them. It is a small sacrifice, after which you can go back to doing what you want."

Nose chimed in, "It's another opportunity for us to demonstrate our superiority."

Although this last remark meant little to them, Mole and Hum didn't have much stamina for an argument and so shrugged their consent.

Nose clasped Hoolow's shoulder. "You did it," he said, "You got the old folks off our backs."

"Yeah," mumbled Mole, "Thanks for getting them off our backs."

Despite their demonstration of pettiness, Hoolow felt their gratitude was genuine, and he reveled in their respect, feeling more a part of them than ever. In fact, if he was honest with himself, he had to admit that he had become the most powerful member of the tribe, holding sway with both the youth and the older members. Without him, there would be no bridge between them, and yet he could not help being disturbed by the youngsters' lack of respect for their elders. Jitters, of course, was the exception; she had a tender love for her mother that was evident. He felt confidence in the others as well. They would grow out of their petulance as he had. But would they? It might take them twice as long as it had taken him, because they encouraged each other in their ideas; or maybe it would take them half as long, because their thoughts worked together.

The next day at the quarry Mole asked Hum, "Why do you think sound affects the spirits the way it does?"

"Dunno," said Hum. He dropped the chert core he'd been chipping and picked up a rough lump to scratch on a nearby boulder. Mole soon joined him in scratching figures on the rock.

Nose looked on but made no sound to stop them; he'd make all the points himself if need be; his points were the best anyway. He looked down at the chocolate brown chert resting on a scrap of leather he had draped over his thigh. With both hands he positioned the tip of the antler against its edge and leaned into it with his chest. A tiny round flake popped off. He moved the antler tip a fraction of its width along the edge and popped off a second flake identical to the first. The work was mechanical; as he performed the motion, his thoughts wandered elsewhere. Not long ago, before Hoolow's return, Mole and Hum had jumped to his command. He counted on their respect. Now it seemed that when they did obey him, it was with humor or distraction. He remembered how he had squeezed himself into the narrow passageway that branched off of the vision room. After crawling until he could go no further, he rolled himself onto his back. The ceiling was a hand's span from his chest, and the walls pressed against his shoulders. A purple deluge poured down waves of fear, and there was no room to thrash. The walls of his confinement began to shatter beneath his fists. Rays of light sliced through the cracks and spread out into fins that warmed the moisture his exertion had created. He was calmed. He rested and noticed how his body felt as if it were configured differently. He pecked at the cracks with the hooked tip of his beak. Pieces of shell broke away, and he looked out over a low valley. He stood to his full height and stretched his wings to either side. He marveled at the amount of space his wings encompassed when he touched their tips before his eyes. He pulled them back, feeling the wind ripple through the long fringe of feathers. He leapt from his perch and soared, enveloped in the even, calming blue of sky. The soft patter of a rabbit browsing through the brush far below caught his attention. He cocked his head to catch sight of it, and its docility stimulated his hunger. He swooped down and captured it with his talons. The rabbit hung limp in his clutches. He released it above an outcrop of sharp rocks, but something happened as he watched it fall: he felt himself tumbling through the air. He flapped, struggling to find the loft that had supported him through his earlier flight, but his agility was sapped; he couldn't fight the plunge. The rocks rose up, and he was once again in darkness—trapped. He pushed against the walls of the passage and managed to scoot himself out with the aid of his feet. The vision had been frightening, but he'd survived it. He felt his power. None of the others had had a vision like his.

Nose looked up at the sound of crunching flint chips and saw the hunters approaching. He cleared his throat to gain Mole and Hum's attention, but they failed to turn until they felt the presence of the men leaning over their shoulders.

Seeing the young men drawing in the full light of day was less than frightening, instead the hunters were puzzled by the activity. Hum was quick to explain, "Here is a deer," he said, as he traced the outline of the animal for the older men. "Can you see?"

The hunters nodded their heads. They could see it, but they couldn't understand the reason for it—why create such a crude representation of what was naturally beautiful and there for the eyes to see in the flesh? They could see no use for such bastardization and couldn't hide their disdain.

Nose stood and extended his piece of antler heavenward. "It's the deer that speaks," he announced and laid his other hand on his chest. The men turned to him. He continued, "The deer tells the shape of the stone it wishes to kill it."

The jaws of the hunters dropped in awe. One spotted the unfinished point partially wrapped in the piece of leather Nose had dropped to the ground. Nose moved his foot to cover it. "The deer does not reveal its secrets to all," he said and admonished them with the back of his hand.

The hunters went away impressed and duped.

Nose was more resentful of Mole and Hum than ever. They had almost lost them the respect of the older men, and here they were chortling over their stupidity, all because the older men could not see what was fascinating in art. "They just don't *get* it," said Mole.

"They are so narrow –"

"—their thinking is so constrained!"

"Stick-brains!"

Yeah, laugh all you want, thought Nose, I know what is important. If you want to leave, leave. With them out of the way, his dominance within the existing tribe would be assured.

Hoolow found in his new partner an inexpressible feeling of connection and bliss, but he was fearful of what anyone witnessing their lovemaking would think—possibly that he was abusing her, causing her harm—when nothing could be further from the truth. It was the play that excited him, knowing he could harm her and yet restraining himself to the very edge, giving her pleasure. Her moans of pleasure excited him almost as much as her feet—how easy it would be to muffle her with a clamped hand—but instead he let her moans ring out, eliciting more and more. This would be proof to the rest of the tribe of his prowess, the only thing he could offer since he was not a hunter. He wanted them to know he was a master at sex, although he could not bear to be seen in the act. They must be careful to keep their trysts private.

When they returned to the rest of the tribe, Hoolow observed the reactions of the elder men, the way their eyes peeled over Jitters skin, perhaps searching for bruises. So, they had heard her screams, but now they seemed satisfied by her health, and they grinned at each other and winked at Hoolow. He felt as if he'd increased in their esteem.

The following morning Jitters and Hoolow strolled near the spring, their fingers entangled and swinging back and forth between them. Jitters leaned in and bumped her hip against Hoolow's. "Hey, *you*," she said.

Hoolow turned to her and smiled.

"You know," she began, and her eyes shifted away.

Hoolow felt his smile dissolve. His heart seemed to rise into his head, its thumps providing a background noise he had to strain to hear through.

"I've been thinking."

Hoolow's mouth went dry. He nodded.

"You know I love being with you." She looked at him earnestly.

Hoolow nodded again.

"But there's something I want to do all by myself."

He could do nothing but stare.

"It's something I've been thinking of since our first visions together in the dark cave, and well, now I feel confident enough to pursue it, but until I know if it's going to work or not, I'd rather not say what it is. You understand, don't you?"

He did not.

"I'm not trying to be secretive or anything. It's just that, well, I need some time to myself. That's all." Her face lost its soft quality.

Hoolow swallowed his urge to protest. He tried to smile, and Jitters giggled. She grabbed his shoulders and leaned in to peck his lips.

As she turned, Hoolow managed to croak, "Where are you going?"

"I really can't say." She tossed it playfully over her shoulder, and as he watched her stride away it was difficult to restrain himself from following. He went to sit by the spring.

Filled with new confidence, Jitters walked alone to the place where the women went to decorate their bodies with sparkling red cinnabar. She'd been the most adept at accentuating the beguiling features of her fellow tribeswomen before becoming bored with the practice, preferring to spend her time gabbing with the other members of her peer set. She had a specific, secret purpose for the cinnabar. The inspiration had flashed through her upon waking from the crushing sleep that followed their collective visions, and she was anxious to see if her idea would work as well as she envisioned it. She hoped that it would secure a greater purpose as well, for although the division between young and old within the tribe seemed to have been breached by Hoolow's fire ceremony, Jitters suspected it would not last. The real difference in the way the two factions perceived their environment was too great.

What she viewed as her mother's simplicity touched her. Her mother's life was a series of responses to her rich environment. Jitters, when she stopped to look, could see much in the environment that was beautiful, that intrigued her, but her thoughts always carried her away from it. She needed to find the thing that could hold her to the spot, the experience of the moment when she knew things were beautiful, as her mother seemed always to be in that place. Jitters would create her own beauty. But she also hoped to show the rest of the tribe, and in so doing, share with them the very nature of the youngsters' visions. She needed to overcome the elders' fear of the dark cave. The intensity of the visions inside frightened them, and she could see why. If not for their extreme beauty, she, too, would be frightened. The elders had no need of these extreme visions, as they spent every moment enmeshed in a subtler sight, seeing everywhere the colored trails sounds and smells left across their path. But since the youngsters had lost this ability, they felt disconnected, not only from their environment but from the rest of the tribe. To Jitters this was a tragedy. Her mother was dear to her. Her mother's grief at the loss of her older sister was still fresh in her memory. She'd done her best to alleviate this grief, and despite her mother's current happiness, she still felt the weight of it.

As she walked, she recalled the scene of her first lovemaking with Hoolow. She had watched his passion with confusion—could toes really be so exciting? She was mystified, but it was entertaining to watch—for a short spell. Just when the boredom was about to make her sigh, he reached up to her calves and pulled himself up, inching over the length of her body, grabbing handholds of her flesh. His firm grips excited her. To her body, he felt possessed in his passion for her. She writhed beneath him, tearing tenderly with her fingers. It was a sort of battle. He could do her such harm, she could feel it in the hardness of his muscles bunching and uncoiling into his thrusts, but instead she felt pleasure wracking her body. She moaned. They stared into each others eyes and ended by laughing.

Hoolow sat by the spring for longer and longer periods, awaiting her return, plagued by images of stalking lions and rock slides tumbling over her. With no one there to help, a simple fall could kill her. When he heard footsteps, he raised his head with expectation, but it was the other four youths; Jitters was not among them. They smirked and trembled with excitement as they exhorted him to come with them to the dark cave.

Jitters stood outside the entrance, her arms wrapped around her chest, but she, too, appeared happy. She released herself and reached out to take Hoolow's hand, leading him through the narrow opening into the second room, where a torch was already waiting. The others piled in behind; they stood in a circle facing each other, the youngsters savoring the sharp zing of complicity. Then Jitters turned to face the wall behind her. She held the torch high. Hoolow stepped to her side. The rest crowded close.

"Do you see it?" she asked excitedly, unable to see his reaction in the dark.

The crystals in the cinnabar reflected the torchlight, tricking his eyes into thinking there was movement in the static image. Hoolow thought he was having a vision. His eyes traced the steady outline of the animal. It was filled with dots. He was awestruck by the genius that had produced it. "How did you do this?" he gasped.

Jitters handed the torch over her shoulder. A leather pouch held the cinnabar she'd pounded to a fine powder. She shook some into the palm of her left hand; she wet her right index finger with spit to lift some of the powder, which she used to draw a line on the cave wall. The simple movements hardly explained the artistry by which she had recreated their vision, for the animal hovered, appearing to undulate in the flickering torchlight. Nipples stood behind, staring hard at the beast. She blinked and shook her head, then backed out, feeling the way behind her with her hands.

As the others emerged from the cave, Nipples winked at the three boys, and they followed her down the slope so that Jitters and Hoolow could be alone.

"My hope is that the paintings will bring the tribe together again, young and old, the way we have not been since before my sister died."

Hoolow's head was still dizzy from viewing her first painting. Her mere words refused to match up with what he had just seen, and he couldn't grasp her meaning.

She tried to clarify, "I made the painting for us, of course, I had little doubt that the others like us would understand, but I also made it for the rest of the tribe. I want to share our vision with them."

"But they are too afraid of the dark cave to ever go in to see it."

"That's just it! I want to alleviate their fear. If we can just get them inside to view the paintings—I plan to do many, many more—then their fears will dissolve. We'll all share the same vision, even if not in the same way. Then the division between us will be healed."

Hoolow was skeptical.

"Nipples and I will paint the visions, exactly as we all saw them together, on every surface. I already have it all laid out." She tapped her temple. "Then we will light the cave. Every part of it will be as bright as day, then how can the rest of the tribe refuse to go in? It is the darkness they fear, since it stimulates visions too intense and also unnecessary to them, because they spend every moment enmeshed in a sort of a vision we young ones have lost the ability to see. But inside the lit cave, they will see the paintings the same way we do. We can all share the same vision, and the division between us will be healed."

Jitters pushed out her cheeks with a broad grin, and the oil on her skin glistened. She was convinced of her eventual success, and it was impossible for Hoolow to resist her enthusiasm. After all, look what she had done with a single painting—the image of it burned in his brain. He could scarcely conceive of what she described—the entire cave painted, every surface, the space lit as bright as daylight—it

151

couldn't be any less than magnificent! If anyone could do this, it would be Jitters. Whether or not the rest of the tribe could be persuaded to view it, he lusted to be dazzled by it. "What do you need me to do?" he asked humbly.

She giggled, "Nothing! Nothing at all, only when it's finished you have to help us convince the rest of the tribe to view it. They respect you. You devised the fire ceremony, and it worked beautifully. You have to think of something like that to lure them to the cave."

"I'm sure I can think of something," he said, and they both fell silent, staring at each other. Jitters' look of satisfaction was precious to him, for he knew it was satisfaction at the thought of what her art might accomplish in bringing the tribe together and not satisfaction in the thing itself, which would have been hubris; he suspected such hubris would be irresistible to him if he'd been the one to create such a thing as the painting. Accomplishment of the thing itself would have an intoxicating affect upon him, rendering him incapable of thinking how it might be put to a worthy purpose—such as bringing the tribe together, something the other youngsters seemed to have no interest in, except possibly Nose, who could see the benefit of it even if it held no sentimental value to him. Jitters alone among the youth still treated her elders with respect. His love for her grew stronger in an instant. "You are a *good* painter," he said.

Just then Nipples and the three boys rejoined them. "Yes," said Nipples, "She is *the* good painter," and she wrapped an arm around Jitters' shoulders, giving her a tight squeeze. "I'm going to help her. Did she tell you? We're going to paint the whole entire cave!"

Hoolow noticed how the boys looked at Jitters with a new respect, and fresh thoughts began squirming through his mind. There was something in himself Hoolow didn't trust.

* * *

Jitters' resemblance to her sister disturbed him in an odd moment. After her first tentative lovemaking, she grew in abandon. Hoolow lay on his back, looking up at her with the moon casting its gray light over her face. He braced his feet in the dirt and thrust into her, but his passion was arrested when she threw her head back and he saw the dark triangle beneath her chin. She took over his rhythm, so that while he lay still, she rocked. He forgot his own pleasure and watched her face go slack with relief, only to clench again as she urged herself to climb the next wave of pleasure. Her expression recalled a scene from his past, one that had burned to his core with shock, humiliation and anger. His memory revived the same emotions, blinding him to the nature of the act in which he was engaged. The emotions seemed to take over, and he clamped his fingers hard on her hips. He drove himself deep inside of her, wanting to reach her very guts and punish her for shaming him when he'd loved her so. Jitters screamed, insensible with ecstasy.

Hoolow groaned and lay limp, while she slipped off of him and slithered up his sweating side to lick his cheek. Her hot tongue stung him, but he restrained himself from flinching. She was not the same, he told himself. He forced himself to look into her face, and he must have looked weary, transformed in some manner, because she giggled and pecked at his lips before snuggling her head into the crook of his neck.

There was no duplicity in this one, he thought. How could there be? They had an understanding, but there was a lingering doubt. Would he be remiss to try to extract a promise from her? Would the words alone be enough? There must be a way to make their intentions toward one another a concrete matter, something outside of themselves. They needed witnesses to their vow. He thought of Nose. It was not hard to see that Nose wished he were in his place at this moment. He saw how Nose watched Jitters kneeling to take a drink from the spring. If Hoolow maneuvered to be on one side of Jitters, there Nose would be on the other. Jitters was so good and kind. If Nose could corner her and make a convincing plea, would she not give in out of tenderness alone? But no, Nose had had ample opportunity to make such a plea during the time Hoolow was away, yet Jitters had taken no lovers. It was her own choice. But perhaps now that she had experienced this sensual pleasure with him, she would be more willing with another. But she was naturally shy! Once again, Hoolow felt the torment of his thoughts. Why wouldn't they stop and allow him the enjoyment of this one precious moment? He rolled to his side, away from Jitters, and stood up. He walked to lean against a dark boulder.

"What is it?" asked Jitters. She'd rolled to her belly and lay propped on her elbows, the moonlight carving a soft pair of crescents from her buttocks.

"Nothing," said Hoolow, but he took secret pleasure from her tone of concern.

Jitters got to her feet and went to his side. She looked closely at his face until he looked away. "What?" she asked.

"I don't know," he said.

"It's something."

"It's just that—I don't know," and he shook his head away from her.

"Tell me."

He felt her hand on his arm. "Well, it's about tomorrow."

"What about it?"

"What about us? Will we be together tomorrow?"

"How can we know?"

"We can make a promise."

Jitters was silent.

"We can promise one another that we will always be together and never be with anyone else the way we have just been with each other."

Jitters looked uneasy.

"Please!" said Hoolow, and he grabbed both her arms, not caring that his desperation was frightening her.

Tears came to her eyes.

Hoolow pulled her to his chest, where he hugged her too fiercely.

"I don't understand," she choked.

"Forget it. Just forget it," he said, releasing her and stalking away.

Jitters leaned back against the rock and cried.

He feared she was too innocent to know how she could harm him. It seemed inevitable to Hoolow that unless they had a binding agreement she would accidentally cause him some harm in the moons to come. He must do whatever he could to guard against it, for her good as well as his own.

But there was more than one reason for Hoolow's desire to proclaim his possession of her: he could see that, at least among the youth, she had leaped ahead of him in respect. The youngsters were in awe of her painting abilities. Hoolow stood to the side, both proud and in awe of her himself, but there was another feeling of which he was ashamed—a jealousy that manifested itself in the fear of losing the esteem of the youth that so intoxicated him. Already, they had drifted out of his control. By joining with Jitters, maybe he could regain some of their respect. He needed to create a formal joining, an illusion of sex for the tribe, but particularly for the youth, that would seal his claim to Jitters. Of course she would continue all of her other activities, the painting in particular. Once he was inextricably associated with her, it

155

would do him the same pride as if he'd done it himself. And he would consecrate her new name, The Good Painter, at the same time. The ritual would be his own artful creation. Just as the animals Jitters drew on the cave wall were representations of their collective visions, the ritual would be a manifestation, a physical declaration of their intentions toward one another, because words were not enough. Words were too abstract and flexible. There had to be witnesses to expand their covenant and make it the responsibility of everyone in the tribe to uphold.

They started at the cracks from which their original visions had issued. They followed the contours of the cave walls, recreating as closely as they could the actual proportions of the magical beasts. As they worked in tandem, The Good Painter maintained a vague awareness of Nipples by her side, as ever, rotating a slender twig between her jaws. She threw down the stick once it had lost the texture her teeth craved. Its wet end glittered with spit, and Good Painter's eyes were drawn to where it lay near the side of her foot. She noticed the way dirt from the bottom of the cave clung to it. She picked it up, shook off the loose brown dirt and rewetted it in her mouth. Then she dragged it through the red pigment and drew it across the wall of the cave. Its wet end created striations of red. Good Painter drew voluptuous curves like the wavy lines that first danced before her eyes at the beginning of a trance. Nipples watched her and then chomped harder on her new twig. Soon its end was another flat, wet brush, and she dipped it into the pigment and imitated Good Painter's sensuous lines. They smiled at one another. It was wonderful. Wouldn't the boys be excited by their invention? Good Painter paused to add some spit to her finger. She smeared one segment of strokes to make a solid contrast and stepped back from her work. Beautiful. She looked over at Nipples, who was concentrating hard. She could use some help.

The Good Painter's thoughts turned to Hoolow. She had no fear of being dominated by him, so why not humor him by participating in the ritual he had devised for their "joining"? She felt her love for him as she smoothed out Nipple's erratic lines. She desired to indulge him, because she feared their sex play may lose some of his passion if she did not acquiesce—and acquiescence was sweet! She envisioned herself lying back on the ground, stretching her arms overhead, remaining limp despite the urge to twist beneath his kisses and bites moving over the length of her as he attempts to tease out a reaction. She turns her head to the side, holding her lips still. He trails his fingertips over her, and she restrains her flinches, compressing them to a deeper level of excitement. She takes perverse pleasure in his growing frustration. He grows forceful to the point she feels overpowered, at which time she unleashes, feeling safe in letting go, knowing he will take her now no matter what. Her limbs spring to clasp him to her, and she can't prevent the moans from escaping.

That night as the tribe sat around the fire, Hoolow stood and clapped his hands to gain everyone's attention. They fell silent, staring curiously at him. He reached down to take The Good Painter's hand and drew her up to stand next to him. Although she'd agreed to Hoolow's notion of a public "joining," she had no idea of how he meant to go about it, and for a moment she was afraid that he meant to take her right there in the midst of the tribe. He placed a hand on each of her shoulders and turned her to face him. Hoolow' eyes were damp, and his lips trembled with seriousness. Realizing that sex in front of the tribe was not his intent, she was awash with relief and had to struggle to pay attention to what he did next, as she knew it was important to him and he wanted her to feel his sincerity. He took a corded bracelet from his wrist and held it up for the rest of the tribe to see. The Good Painter looked along with the rest, still not understanding his purpose. He gazed back at her, and it took a moment for her to realize what he wanted and to hold out her arm, her hand in a loose fist. He slipped the bracelet over the fist and tightened it around her wrist. He bent to tear the loose string with his teeth; a drop of his saliva tingled against her skin. Hoolow embraced her. He put a proud arm around her waist and turned back to the rest of the tribe, whose looks of curiosity persisted. "This is one body now," he said, making eye contact with all of the men in the shelter, young and old alike. For the benefit of the young ones, he said, "The Good Painter and I are now one." The Good Painter smiled and suppressed a giggle. His gravity was comical to her. When Hoolow and The Good Painter sat down, the rest of the tribe shrugged and resumed their earlier conversations—it was just Hoolow after all. The Good Painter was well satisfied. It was done, and as she expected, the ceremony left her with no particular feeling, only the same old love she'd felt for Hoolow before, but he looked on her with eyes filled with gratitude. She'd done him a favor, and she could see that he appreciated it. Now that his insecurity had been smoothed over, she could focus on painting the cave.

Within a single cycle of the moon, the walls of the first room were finished, and she needed a means to reach the ceiling. Naturally, she went to Nose with this problem.

Nose reconstructed the layout of the cave in his imagination; he moved through it, seeing every angle without taking a step. There were many rocks suitable for piling to reach the ceiling, but he dismissed this idea. The Good Painter and Nipples needed to move around, and constructing and deconstructing a mound of rocks would be too cumbersome for them. They required something maneuverable—a tree without roots or rather two trees with branches in between. All the excess branches, the ones that got in the way, could be stripped away. This would be light enough for the girls to move on their own.

Nose solicited the help of Mole and Hum. The three boys chipped at the trunks of a pair of slender trees with handaxes. After the trees toppled, Nose directed Mole and Hum to hold them upright, while he paced between the two. Of course, he could add new roots to the shorn trunks. That would keep them vertical. He looked to their tops. The branches could be made to intertwine, thus giving The Good Painter a place to recline while she painted the ceiling, but with only one point of attachment at either end she'd be likely to sway with every movement. How would she be able to complete her work under such conditions? He looked back to the tree butt Mole had planted between his feet. Ah, two trees on either side would solve both problems: a stable base and an unswaying platform for The Good Painter.

"We'll need two more, boys."

"Are you sure?" asked Hum. He wiped the sweat from his brow with a dramatic swipe of the back of his hand.

"Yes, I'm sure," said Nose and walked to where a handaxe had been left in the dirt. He hacked the next trunk.

Mole laid down his tree and went to join him.

"What can I do?" asked Hum.

"Why don't you start stripping off all those branches?"

"I thought you were going to weave them together."

"I've thought of something else."

"What?"

"Don't worry about it, okay. Just do it."

Hum grumbled as he scanned the ground for a suitable stone. Finding one, he raised it above his head and smashed it to the rock at the base of the slope below the dark cave, where it shattered. He picked amongst the broken pieces, selecting one with a flat edge appropriate for scraping. He sat, fitted the cut end of the tree against his belly and held its trunk between his feet. He scraped the flat end of the stone shard down the trunk, shaving off the small branches, rotating the tree as he went.

Mole and Nose felled the third tree. "Don't mess up the bark," said Nose. "I want some long strips."

"Yeah," said Hum. He didn't look up from his task.

The three worked quietly together, and the scene had some of the feel of the old days, the days before Hoolow; Nose was glad of it.

Before long, all three boys sat shearing the branches from the freshly cut trees that released their sap onto their hands.

"What shall we do with these branches?" asked Hum.

"Pile them over there."

Hum rose with an armful, but when he attempted to release them, one stuck to either hand. "They won't let me go," he said, shaking his hands in frustration.

Nose and Mole looked up and laughed.

Hum redoubled his efforts, this time for show, and it had the desired affect. All three laughed until, finally, Mole got up and pulled the branches from Hum's hands.

When the two pairs of bare trees lay side by side and there was a pile of branches and two stacks of bark strips, Nose was satisfied.

"What now?" asked Hum.

"We'll use the bark strips to lash the trunks together, like attaching points to spear shafts only we'll leave a gap, see." And he began to arrange the parts on the ground.

"I don't see how the girls will be able to reach the ceiling that way."

Nose blew the air out of his nostrils, but he managed to control the tone of his voice, "First we will lash these two together. Then we will lash these other two together. Finally, we will lash the two pairs together, and then it will stand upright, like two people holding hands."

Mole and Hum looked at him skeptically, but they set about following his instructions. Nose took great satisfaction in their amazed expressions as they held the two sides of the scaffold while he affixed the crossed braces that strengthened the construction.

"Okay," he said, grabbing hold of a pair of braces and giving them a good shake: there was hardly a rattle. It worked as well in reality as it did in his thoughts, and he congratulated himself on his ingenuity, thinking, I am smarter than Hoolow, who is all words. Why can't she see? Why does she prefer him to me? "Let's get this thing up to the cave," he said gruffly.

Nose walked ahead of the other two, who carried the scaffold between them. Reaching the top, Nose looked back. Although Mole and Hum had to lift the scaffold high to clear the rocky path, they did not appear to struggle. It would be a cinch for the girls. Mole and Hum set the scaffold down before him.

"Inside," he said, gesturing into the cave.

Mole and Hum followed his command wordlessly. Nose was already on his way down the slope to get the branches he intended for the top of the scaffold. He had an armful by the time Mole and Hum rejoined him. "No, no," he said, "I'll finish up myself. You can go now."

"You sure?"

Nose nodded without an upward glance. He was scarcely aware of their footfalls trailing away as he carried his armload of branches, soft ones he imagined cradling The Good Painter, to the cave. He interwove the branches across the top of the scaffold, wishing she were still Jitters, but even he could see that the name no longer suited her. She was not the same girl. Nipples now looked to her for direction.

Nose stood back to admire his work.

The Good Painter's delighted squeal made him jump. She raced around him and launched herself onto the scaffold. Nose laughed. Needing no instruction on how to reach the platform, she found easy holds on the crossed braces. At the top, she threw herself down on the soft branches, and the scaffold barely shook. She leaned her head over the side and smiled down at Nose. "It's perfect!" she said gleefully and flopped back, miming brushstrokes on the ceiling.

Nose watched her hands fall back to her chest. She sank deep in the branches so that he could not see her, only the shape of her body from below, and she was still. He said to himself, she's thinking, and his heart fluttered. Suddenly she sat up, then lowered herself down the opposite side of the scaffold. Nose's eyes tracked her as she went to collect her paints. Passing by him, she said, "Thank you, Nose," and it sounded formal and disinterested.

Rather than offense, Nose felt a certain kinship with her concentration. He related her creative intent to how he had felt during the construction of the scaffold, and sensing the possibility for a new level of connection between them, he meant to tell her so. "Jitters," he began.

Before he could go on, she said sharply, "Call me Good Painter. I never liked that other name."

All that he'd intended to say evaporated. Of course, she was The Good Painter. He felt ashamed and didn't know why. For a moment he'd forgotten Jitters had a new name, one the others seemed to remember without a thought, never accidentally calling her by the old name as he had just done, insulting her. Should he tell her he was sorry? He saw that she was already engrossed in her work. His apology would only be an interruption.

As he walked away, he thought with admiration how The Good Painter always knew what the next move should be in regards to painting the cave. She and Nipples were obsessed with painting. More than Mole and Hum, who doodled on rocks and spent hours philosophizing meanings for the sparest visions, The Good Painter and Nipples had created a larger vision from the conglomeration of all of their smaller ones. It encompassed the entire cave—their intention had become clear to him. The Good Painter had thought out every part of it, and Nipples was in thrall to her artistic vision. She'd lost all interest in Mole and Hum, and had even stopped trying to entice Hoolow, as if the marriage ceremony had worked its magic primarily on her. Now it appeared that Nipples followed The Good Painter around, absorbing her every word and direction. Even Hoolow, whom Nose once presumed would usurp their current leader, his well-known former rival, was fading into the background of The Good Painter's power. Her art was so evocative—how could anyone resist? If the rest of the tribe could ever be led into the cave, if they were ever to see what she had done there, then there would be no limit to her power. But he doubted that that could ever happen. The elders were too entrenched in their old way of seeing; they would never consent to enter the dark cave.

The disintegrating carcass of a buzzard caught his eye. Its black feathers were scattered over the plain, some of them fluttering, pinned to the ground by a gnarled bit of bone. As he surveyed the carnage, a downy underfeather caught a breeze and spiraled into the air. Its wispy revolutions stirred an idea in his brain. He bent to pick up one of the long, stiff tail feathers and drew its edge across the first coarse whiskers to grace his cheek. He grinned as he ran, collecting an armload of feathers. He stuffed them into a crevice between two boulders and rolled a smaller rock in front to hide them.

He knew where to find Hum and Mole. They'd made it a daily habit to meet in a field of basalt blocks not far from the spring. There they scratched on the rocks with abandon, and the women knew to stay away. Nose found them reclining in the shade, not talking, and with their eyes half-closed. To Nose they appeared as vacant as any of the older men. He approached, taking his time so that he could make note of the changes in their appearances. Hum had a distinct growth on his upper lip and some signs on his chin, but his cheeks were still smooth. Mole's facial hair was thin and patchy. Nose noticed it with satisfaction. He affected a casual air and strode up to the two meditators, stroking his cheek as if it were a mere absentminded gesture. Mole blinked at the sound of his footfalls and looked up, smiling a greeting. "Hey, man," said Hum.

Nose hadn't considered what to say; mostly he had wanted to be noticed, and having accomplished that, he dropped into a comfortable squat. The three young men, long accustomed to each other's company, remained quiet. After a few moments, the eyelids of Mole and Hum descended halfway, and Nose was offended by what he thought of as their withdrawal from his companionship. Feeling detached and wanting their conversation, he said, "Hey." Their eyelids shot up, and Nose rushed on, eager to hold their attention, "What would you think if I changed my name like The Good Painter?"

"You're not a painter," said Hum.

"No, I would choose something else, more suited to me."

Mole and Hum were nonplussed.

"Come on, what do you think? What do I look like?" and he turned his face to give them a view of his profile.

No response.

"Anything? Look," and he drew a fingertip over the arch of his great nose.

"Nose," the other two said affectionately.

"Anything else?" he said in exasperation.

They looked at him helplessly

"Doesn't it look like a beak? Don't I look like some kind of bird? A Hawk, maybe?"

Mole leaned closer, squinting at Nose's profile, and Nose held his face still for his inspection. Hum began to nod. "Yeah," he said, "I can sort of see that. That's cool, man."

Mole sat back, saying, "Sure, I can see it. Hawk, huh? You want that to be your name?"

Nose had hoped for a more dramatic proclamation of his new moniker. He felt dissatisfied. He prodded them, "What about you guys? Don't you want new names?"

The two looked at each other and back at Hawk. Hum spoke for the both of them, "What we've got is fine."

"Fine," said Hawk, getting to his feet. He wasn't out of earshot before looking back at the other two, who were already lost in meditation. His thoughts turned to his stash of feathers. He was going to need many more, and they would be for himself alone. It was time for him to concentrate on furthering his own best interest.

He scouted for more feathers, adding to his stash until it began to overflow and his thoughts turned to constructing a frame to hold them. He remembered how he'd built the scaffold, and this time he chose flexible branches, bending them into the shape of a wing and adding the same sort of crossed braces, only lighter; he wove the feathers through, noting where there were gaps he needed to fill. He worked with no sense of urgency. The girls were still working everyday at painting the cave. Mole and Hum spent more and more time sitting amongst the basalt blocks, small lumps of rock lying in their slack hands. Hawk missed the sound of their restless chatter. He wasn't used to so much time alone. When he grew lonely, he went in search of the other boys, hoping to rouse them to conversation, as he remembered many happy days of times past, when they'd played and encouraged each other, sharing thoughts that led to innovations in the tools they'd made for pleasure. It wasn't so much a chore forced upon them then as it was now, seeming mundane. He'd never kept a secret from them before, and he felt guilty as he approached their company.

He found them bathing in the spring. Hum spotted him and called out with gusto, "Nose, Nose!"

Mole squinted in his direction and raised a welcoming hand.

Hawk was happy to see his fellows but disappointed that they'd so soon forgotten his new name. His first impulse was to let it go and dive in, but instead he drew himself up. If he meant to have their respect, then he must establish himself. He shook off his feeling of sheepishness and stopped at the edge of the spring. Placing his hands on his hips, he looked down on the other two. "Name's Hawk," he said, and he meant for his voice to sound neutral, but it sounded stern.

Hum angled the edge of his palm just below the surface of the water and spun himself around, sending up a tall white wing that splashed over Hawk, wetting him from hair to toes. Hawk reeled back in surprise, shaking the water from his ears in time to hear Mole throw back his head and shout the great screeching call of a hawk in flight. As he did so, he slapped the surface of the water with his open hands, sending up small white sprays, mockingly small.

There was a moment of shock, during which Hawk absorbed the idea that he was being ridiculed. Hum and Mole were just as shocked to see him turn away. They hadn't received the laughter and retaliation their act had meant to provoke. Hum leapt from the water and ran dripping after him, catching him by the arm in a wet grip. Hawk spun and was surprised again when he noticed Hum now stood taller than he did.

"Hey, man, Hawk, no offense, hey?" said Hum in a conciliatory tone, but Hawk was holding tight to his feeling of affront. He turned his hard eyes to Hum's hand still clutched to his upper arm. Hum let his hand drop and watched Hawk walk away. His sadness only lasted a moment before he turned back and threw himself in the water with a wild whoop. Mole cheered. Hawk heard their frenetic splashes as further insults to his dignity.

He returned to his hidden wing, and drawing it out of its cubby, he added a few more feathers before laying it aside with a sigh. Perhaps the girls wouldn't mind some company. He hid the wing and walked around its hiding place, making sure no feathers showed, then he started in the direction of the dark cave.

From amongst a pile of rocks at the bottom of the slope, he heard a masculine voice followed by a high feminine one. He concealed himself and trained his ears to listen. It was Hoolow and The Good Painter. She was doing most of the talking, "We're getting close, and listen, I know it probably doesn't make much sense to you, but I want to make the cave off-limits until we're ready to show it to the whole tribe together."

"But why?" asked Hoolow.

Hawk climbed higher, careful where he put each foot lest the rolling of a single pebble give away his presence. He found a hiding place with a view that looked down on the couple. They reclined on separate rocks, facing one another; their bodies stretched out so that the soles of their feet pressed together and their toes entwined; their hands lay curled on their bellies.

The Good Painter was saying, "It might be a silly notion, but I want you and Mole and Hum and Nose (Hawk cringed at the sound of his old name) to feel the impact of seeing it finished at the same time as the rest. I know it won't be as –" she paused, "wonderful –" and she flicked her eyes over to Hoolow. There was no change in his expression. She continued, "As it will be for the rest of the tribe, seeing it for the first time, but maybe you'll feel something of it if you haven't seen it every step of the way."

"I guess I can understand that," said Hoolow, and he squeezed her toes with his.

She giggled, and Hoolow rolled in her direction, reaching for her.

Hawk slunk away with less care than he'd approached, knowing they were less inclined to hear. He felt the need to inform Mole and Hum of what he'd just heard, and this time he found them drying themselves on the rocks by the spring. Hawk went and stood over them. Hum opened his eyes a crack and lifted a hand to shield the sun as he looked up at Hawk. "Hey, you came back," he said and nudged Mole with his elbow.

Mole, who was lying on his stomach, turned on his side and cocked his arm to rest his cheek on his hand. "What's up, Hawk?" he said with measured casualness so that Hawk knew that he meant it as an apology, and the bad feeling he'd held against him washed away.

"You know what," Hawk began, and he crossed his arms high over his chest to demonstrate his defiance, "The Good Painter means to bar us from the dark cave."

Their reaction was slight. "How do you know that?" asked Hum. He sat up and scooted backward until he could lean against a rock.

Hawk added sharpness to his voice, still hoping to incite them, "I just overheard her talking to Hoolow."

Hum shrugged. Mole turned his eyes to Hum, then back to Hawk. "To tell the truth," he said, "we were kind of getting bored with it anyway."

Hawk dropped his arms and his jaw at the same time— "B-bored"—his brief stutter drew him back to his composure. He re-crossed his arms over his chest, but this time they hung loose. He couldn't think of what to say; his eyes peeled over the rocks next to the spring and saw that the mud they'd used to cover Mole and Hum's original drawings was crackled and flaking, revealing some of their lines. Hawk stooped, scooped fresh mud from the edge of the spring and smoothed it over the gaps. The other two watched with dumbfounded expressions. When he'd finished, he stepped back to survey his work, and without another look at Mole and Hum, he walked away. He heard his name called, "Hawk?" but he kept walking, wondering how such a gulf had managed to open between them. Of course, they'd not had the kind of vision he'd had in the deep narrow passage. Maybe that was what it was, or if he was honest with himself—they'd never been as smart as he was, and now to add to their deficiency, they'd become lazy and uninterested in making new tools. Well, if they wanted to split the tribe, he'd help them.

It was twilight as Hawk picked his way toward where he'd earlier seen Hoolow and The Good Painter. As he suspected, they were no longer there, most likely returned to the shelter to eat with the rest of the tribe. Nipples, too, would be there, which meant the cave was empty. He entered and stood for a few moments in the dark, examining the change in the cave's air. The dank musty smell had grown other dimensions since he'd last visited. The girls kept it lit for long periods while they did their painting, and the astringent smell of fresh charcoal was heavy, but there was another, animal scent to the place. The women had worked hard, alone, in the close space, and the female odor they left behind was pure, untinged by the male sweat that permeated the shelter. It mingled with the metallic smell of their recent menses and the raw meat smell of their groins that made him salivate and imagine himself licking between their labia. He wanted to douse himself in their scent. He breathed in, excited.

He struck flint against a chunk of iron pyrite to get a spark; it was his own method of which he was proud. He lit his torch and lifted it to illuminate a patch of ceiling. A pair of bulls faced each other, their horns interlocking but with no sense of struggle. He moved his torch to see the rest of their bodies appearing to float in the air; the painting's likeness to their visions made his knees tremble. The cinnabar sparkled, and the black charcoal spots that circled the bulls' bodies seemed to oscillate in the penumbra of light. His torch popped; he felt it jerk in his hand and dropped it. It fell in front of his feet, nearly singeing his toes and causing him to jump back from it in fright. He forced a laugh as he bent to pick it up. He took note of the scaffold standing against one wall. They'd moved it easily and were still using it. His design served its intended purpose, and he grinned to himself with satisfaction.

He stepped to the far wall and tried to hold the torch steady as he walked, illuminating the animals that seemed to issue from the cracks. The Good Painter had used the natural undulations of the rock to give the animals depth and form. A rock protuberance became a bull's hump. A deer's leap fit neatly in a recess. It took him several passes around the room to realize that all of the animals, save the two bulls facing off in the middle of the ceiling, faced the vertical opening at the back. He stepped through, firming his grip on the torch. In the second, smaller room, the animals were closer together. They faced in all directions, overlapping one another as they did when the visionaries sang most frantically. He grew dizzy as he turned, trying to follow the outlines of individual animals, his eyes catching onto the lines of the next one and carrying him on. He turned and turned. He went to his knees and felt along the floor, his fingers seizing on a soft nodule. He brought it close to his face and held his torch over it. He saw how the charcoal blackened his hand and knew it was what he was looking for.

He braced his torch between two rocks and crawled into the narrow passage. When he could go no further, he turned onto his back. His eyes were open, but it made no difference. He breathed out and felt the warm breath redirected to his cheeks by the ceiling that was a nose-length in front of his face. The purple outline of a figure appeared above him. He tried to reach out for it, but his hand was stopped by the ceiling. He brought up the charcoal; the lack of space dictated that his elbow stay bent, thus constraining his movement so that he had to concentrate to trace over the outline, the charcoal erasing the purple line as it went, which was okay, because Hawk knew he was leaving his permanent mark on the cave. The Good Painter may have the rest of the cave, but this one place of power would be his. He started at the head; it was the profile of a mighty bird, a bird of prey with a thick, hooked beak. He made his line over it, watching it disappear as he went. As he traced the line over its neck, the figure began to change. Instead of spreading out into wings, it sloped down and went straight. He was so focused on tracing the outline, he at first didn't realize it was changing shape; it was not until he was tracing over the second leg, parallel to the first and descending from the straight body, that he knew he was drawing a man. It was too late to correct it. The purple outline had already been obliterated by his black lines. He could never find where to start again. All that remained were the purple man's feet, glowing before him. He drew over them the five spreading claws of a hawk. He retreated from the passage as quickly as he could, leaving the charcoal behind.

His torch had gone out, so he knew the second room by its greater space alone. He was eager to get out. He felt along the walls to the crack that led to the outer room; he stumbled through and out into the night lit with stars. He knew the rest of the tribe must never be allowed to enter; he would loose everything if they did. He had to best The Good Painter now or lose his opportunity forever, because her power, as that of all women, increased with age, while that of the men, damaged from long hunts, slowly waned—if they managed to escape being gored by an injured bull. He recalled how he'd once assumed his place at the top was assured: he simply had to wait for enough of the older men to die, and he would step up. It would have been as easy as that before Hoolow arrived. But now he saw his place in the tribe, as a master inventor and craftsman, being pushed to the side, because Hoolow's power had transformed Jitters into The Good Painter, and now she stood to rise into top position. His once shy girlfriend now appeared to be a woman of unstoppable powers, and he couldn't countenance being subject to her for the rest of his life.

*   *   *

The Good Painter stayed after Nipples had gone. She'd stayed to the last possible moment, and Hoolow was most likely already worried and on his way to meet her so that she would not have to walk through the dark alone. Splattered with paint, she hurried down the slope, so he would not have to come the whole way, and she came face to face with Hawk. Both were surprised by the other and stopped, eyes locked.

Hawk felt a spark jump the space between them. They exchanged the exact look as when they were two children and understood each other as individuals, apart from all the others. The promise of those long ago moments welled up in him; he flooded with hope. She was the same Jitters as ever. Perhaps recently she had forgotten, but in this moment she remembered everything, all that they had shared since the beginning, and it would be as it was between them. He watched the corners of her mouth lift into a smile, and he felt his eyes go moist with relief—Jitters! He'd decided to tell her his plan and offer her the chance to rule by his side, which was more than Hoolow could offer, when he heard her name called.

"Good Painter," called Hoolow, "There you are!"

Hawk watched her turning toward the voice, severing their connection without hesitation. He stepped back into the shadows. Hoolow reached out to The Good Painter, and she raced into his embrace. "I was worried," Hawk heard him say, and The Good Painter laughed. Hoolow braced an arm around her shoulders and began to guide her in the direction of camp. She looked back over her shoulder, searching for Hawk in the shadows, but he stayed hidden. She did not look for long. Hawk went to retrieve his wings.

Nipples sang her song with words, the others—Mole, Hum, and The Good Painter—joining in one by one. They sang with their eyes closed, which was in itself mysterious to the rest of the tribe, who liked to watch their songs as well as listen to them. They could not understand what the youngsters were doing. It sounded like singing, but the elders didn't know which they were supposed to listen to: words or melody. How could they enjoy the melody, pretty as it was— Nipples was a good improviser—when it was adulterated with meanings? Those misplaced meanings grated on their nerves, causing confusion until all they heard was noise, and it was about to become intolerable.

The old mother watched her daughter singing, her eyes closed, and she felt afraid. She did not recognize the creature before her. It was something of inscrutable ways. She had been infected with something. Her body was speckled with random flecks of paint as if she'd allowed herself to be decorated by the whitebeard, when once her daughter had been a master at creating beautiful designs on the bodies of the other women. This disintegration of her talents was indicative of disease, along with the noise she was singing, if it could be called singing at all.

The once young hunter watched the old mother examining her daughter. He studied the concern that coursed across her features. He felt likewise, but he needed to know if she would object to the driving out of these others. She still held the tightest bond to any of the youths, but the depth of their aberration had reached a point where her connection could be severed without too much grief. It would be grief for the dead, a common enough thing.

The stones' voices had quieted as he'd come to depend on the youths' stones, and yet he was confident that if he concentrated, he would hear them calling again. He'd studied the stones of the youth, and although it had been long since he'd asked the grandmother for help in interpreting the voices of stones, he'd once been an adept. His eyes caught those of the old mother, and there was an understanding between them. Already he could see her pain, and he pitied her. He would do all that he could to comfort her after the deed was done. He was unaware of the Hawk stalking toward them.

The Hawk stretched his wings and felt his strength. He marveled at the weight of his feathers, blacker than the surrounding darkness. They rippled over his bones. He lifted his shoulders, and his wings fanned out to either side, creating a massive shadow. He was prepared to eat death. He slunk to the shelter and managed to skirt into the shadows unnoticed. The scene was as he feared: the youths were singing, and the elders watched them with rapt attention. It would not be long before they were persuaded to visit the dark cave. Hawk took a moment to gloat over the bedevilment of their plans before crashing into their midst with a piercing screech, wingtips touching above his head.

He was a creature like they'd only seen before in their dreams, an incredible beast, half-bird, half-man, with giant flapping black wings. The formerly young hunter stretched out a shaking hand to touch a feather, confirming that it was real and no confusion of the senses brought about by the confounding song of the youth, who were now standing, gazing at the beast in horror and identifying it for the others—"Hawk! Hawk!" They stood their ground as the rest of the tribe scuttled to the back of the shelter. The elders and their young children looked out at the illuminated figures circling the fire. The Hawk spread its wings, and the elders gasped. This was what the youth had done with their secret goings on in the dark cave. This devil was what Hoolow had brought into their midst.

Hoolow was talking to the great bird, "Hawk, what are you doing, you'll ruin everything!"

175

The beast turned toward those huddled in the back. Extending one mighty wing at Hoolow, he proclaimed, "This one has brought discord to the tribe. This one has corrupted the youth and conjured spirits."

The Good Painter stepped forward. "It's not true!" she shouted. She turned to Hawk, "No, Hawk, don't do this! Why are you doing this? You're ruining it!" She could not see his grimace beneath the two flaps of bark he'd fashioned into a beak, but his eyes were stolid.

The once young hunter was riveted to the scene before him. It dawned on him that the Hawk's arrival was the manifestation of his own intention. He picked up his spear and went to stand behind the beast. The others followed suit until all were standing in opposition to Hoolow and the youth.

The Good Painter cried on Hoolow's shoulder. "No," she said as if to herself, "it's not supposed to be this way." She turned to Hawk. The tears on her cheek sparkled in the firelight as she stepped forward, reaching out a hand to him. He slapped it away with his wingtip. The hunters pounded the butts of their spears against the floor of the shelter in unison. The Good Painter stepped back.

Hoolow realized there wasn't much time to linger. He took his last sad look at the faces before him, searching in vain for the one who wasn't there—where was the whitebeard? He raked his eyes over the back of the shelter, spotting a single slight figure lying on its side. He went to him, squatted and laid a hand on the boney shoulder that responded with warmth. The whitebeard sat up, alert and not as if rising from sleep; it was as if he'd merely been disinterested in the spectacular goings on in the shelter. Hoolow groped for his hand in the dark, saying, "Come." The dark shape of the whitebeard's head shook from side to side. The rhythm of spear butts pounding on the floor accelerated. Their urgency tickled the bottoms of Hoolow's feet. "Come!" he commanded. But the dark head continued to shake, and Hoolow could just make out the faint sound of the old man's chuckle above the drumming spears. He stood and stepped away. The old mother came and knelt behind the whitebeard. Hoolow watched as the old man reclined against her breasts, and she wrapped her arms around him. Hoolow passed by Hawk without a word. The group of youngsters—Mole and Hum and Nipples and The Good Painter—huddled together as they watched Hoolow descend from the shelter. After a few moments they followed him to the dark cave, the pursuing tattoo of spear butts fading in their wake.

The entrance was piled with fodder for the huge illuminating fires they had intended to build. They constructed one giant pyre in the first chamber. Mole and Hum were the first to attack the scaffold. They tugged at its braces and were surprised at how tenaciously they stuck together. They couldn't help but admire Hawk's design even while hell-bent on destroying it. They were grateful when Hoolow and the women joined in the destruction. Together they rocked and twisted the scaffold. Whenever a piece came free, they hurled it onto the fire, releasing some venom into the flames. Finally, the top branches fell at their feet, and they scooped them in their arms and flung them over the flames that leapt to consume them in a crackling flash of sparks.

"Son of a bitch!" screamed Hum.

Mole threw back his head and howled in fury. Hoolow and the women joined him in venting their anger at Hawk. Every one seethed at the thought of The Good Painter's frustrated ambition. She was the first to fall silent. The others looked to her and noticed her eyes panning over the cave walls. They watched her beautiful creations leaping and jumping in the lambent light. The popping and hissing of flames became the bellows of cows and the hot snorted breath of bulls facing off, scratching the unseen ground with their hooves. The Good Painter began to weep, and Hoolow was the first to put his arms around her. The others gathered round, laying a hand on her wherever they could.

"It's beautiful," said Nipples, "more beautiful than I imagined it could be."

"Beautiful," murmured the others.

"All for nothing," mumbled The Good Painter.

They responded with a chorus of "nos."

"This room has power," said Hoolow, "too much power. Can't you feel it?" His eyes sought those of the ones standing by, and they nodded, chancing glances over their shoulders as it appeared the animals may detach from the wall at any second and trample their heads.

The Good Painter wiped the tears from her eyes. She looked at her work and felt her heart pound with recognition of her success. She quelled it by reminding herself of the failure of her ultimate intent.

The group was weary from the night's events. Hoolow and The Good Painter lay down next to the fire; Nipples lay between the two other men on the opposite side. None could sleep. Their eyes stayed open, staring up at the animals who ranged overhead, for whenever the humans closed their eyes, they saw the paintings charge into action, and their eyes sprang open to confirm that the paintings had not moved. This forced vigilance made them restless. Hum sat up. Happy to be distracted from the paintings, the others turned to him. "I can't take this," he said, meeting their raw eyes and seeing that they were ready for suggestions.

"What can we do?" asked Mole.

Hum paused for a long moment. He looked at The Good Painter and sounded apologetic when he said, "Let's kill them."

The Good Painter's eyes grew wide.

"The paintings," said Hum, "Let's kill the paintings."

The Good Painter looked to the faces of the ones sitting across the fire. Each nodded, Nipples with the tracks of tears sliding down her cheeks. The Good Painter's eyes locked with Hoolow's, and she felt his sympathy. His chin dipped, and she dropped her head. She allowed herself a moment to mourn before she got to her feet. She extracted a fresh lump of charcoal from the edge of the firepit. It was still warm in her hand. She walked to the wall and stood in front of a graceful doe, one she remembered painting; the memory of the twig brush in her hand caused her fingers to flex. She admired the way the spots she'd dabbled across its flank suggested the undulation of muscle in the firelight, and then, with a single stroke of the charcoal, she sent a spear into its chest. The doe convulsed and fell to the floor with a spew of blood from its nostrils. The others dug through the embers for appropriate weapons.

Nipples stood poised in front of a bull, the hand that held the charcoal raised and shaking as she looked to The Good Painter, who stepped to her side, and clasping her hand over Nipples' shaking one, slashed the charcoal over the beast's throat. The bull heaved itself to the ground with a final gasp of breath.

Hoolow offered his two hands laced together for Mole to use as a step for climbing onto Hum's shoulders. From this perch, Mole reached up to massacre the two greatest bulls, who crumpled together in death, raining blood. Gruesome clouds gathered into a thunderstorm fueled by the lightning flashes and cracks from the fire. To escape the gory deluge, the hunters took up torches and made their way through the narrow slit into the second chamber, where the bloodletting became frenzied. They leapt against the walls, flinging their charcoal spears every which way as it was hard to distinguish individual animals in the galloping jumble. The hunters tore their knuckles against the rock and slipped in the blood that wetted the cave floor. Their rapid exhalations filled the chamber with sound, and they grew still with listening. They stood with their backs together, torches in front of their chests, turning as they examined the walls, noticing that every beast had been skewered by multiple charcoal thrusts. They let their weapons drop from their hands and wiped their fingers against their sides. Bearing these wounds of battle, they made their way back to the first chamber, The Good Painter in front. She threw her torch onto the withering flame and watched it flare. The others followed suit, waiting for The Good Painter to sit before sitting themselves. Hoolow was by her side. The other three sat opposite. They stared into the fire until their eyelids drooped. Hoolow felt The Good Painter slump against his side, and he lowered her to the floor. He curled his body around her, although there was no longer any threat from the animals she'd painted.

In the morning he found her sitting outside with her back to the mouth of the cave. The others were still asleep. He sat down beside her. "We'll find another cave," he whispered.

She stared out at the pinkening horizon.

"You can paint again."

"Of course I will," she said and turned her face to him; a struggle between sadness and amusement was taking place behind her eyes. Hoolow squeezed her tight, and they waited for the late sleepers to arise.

* * *

Inside the cave, Nipples awoke from a heart-pounding dream. Mole and Hum were still asleep on either side of her, and so she waited for her blood to calm before extricating herself from between the two. She heard The Good Painter and Hoolow whispering outside. It wouldn't be long before they grew impatient; she had to move fast. She squeezed herself through the narrow opening at the back of the chamber and paused to accustom herself to moving in darkness. Her hands would have to do the work here. With effort, she got to her knees and began pushing rocks toward the opening of the small passageway. She moved as quietly as possible, for once regulating her breath, until she felt confident that the opening was secured. Her skin was slick from the effort and caused a shiver in the cool darkness. She pushed herself to her feet and smoothed her hands through her long hair. Perhaps she'd let The Good Painter braid it later. She returned to Mole and Hum, now sleeping face to face, each with an arm slung around the other's waist. She smiled before kicking Mole's buttocks. "Up, slugabeds! It's a whole new world out there," she said and went to join the couple waiting outside.

As soon as Hum and Mole emerged, rubbing the sleep from their eyes, the troop headed off in the direction opposite the tribe's shelter.

"How about some grub?" said Hum, and the others laughed.

"In time," said Hoolow.

At mid-morning they stopped to rest. The Good Painter stooped to dig a depression in the dirt so that Nipples could sit more comfortably. Nipples smiled as she lowered herself and leaned back against a boulder. The Good Painter joined her in massaging her high, round belly.

ACKNOWLEDGMENTS

I knew when I first read Julian Jaynes's book, *The Origin of Consciousness in the Breakdown of the Bicameral Mind*, over a decade ago that the ideas it contained would make a great fiction, but *Thrall* didn't begin to crystallize until I read *The Mind in the Cave* by David Lewis-Williams. I'm most grateful for these two authors and their books.

I owe a deep debt of gratitude to Kathryn Wilham. Her many pages of notes on an early draft of *Thrall* were invaluable to me when revising the manuscript. Any deficiencies in the final version are, of course, my fault.

Many thanks to Eric T. Reynolds without whom this book wouldn't exist.

Thanks to the Maturango Museum for a great tour of Little Petroglyph Canyon, China Lake. Thanks to archaeologist and friend, Dave Nichols, for a day spent driving me around the Mojave and to Jeff Putzi, who made that drive all the more enjoyable (I told you I'd work you in).

Thanks to another great friend, archaeologist and artist, Gregg Cestaro, for creating some great cover art.

Thanks to Stacy Danielle Stephens and to Terri-Lynne DeFino for excellent proofreading.

Special thanks to Randy, Charlene and Ed for their enthusiastic support of my work.

And, finally, to all of my many family members and friends not already mentioned, there's not enough room here to express my gratitude.

Peace to all.

March 2010

ABOUT THE AUTHOR

Kimberly Todd Wade earned a degree in anthropology from the University of Miami and performed graduate studies at Tulane University. She worked as an archaeologist for fourteen years, including field work in Belize, Hawaii, and Palau. Her novella, *Making Love in Madrid*, was published in 2007.